"Humorous, sizzling hot, romantic, and not missing dramatics. If you weren't a fan before, you certainly will be after reading *Rusty Nailed*."

—*Love Between the Sheets*

"Excuse me, I need to catch my breath. Either from panting or cracking up. Because I was always doing one of the two while reading *Rusty Nailed*. Alice Clayton, you never disappoint."

—*Book Bumblings*

"Simon and Caroline are as adorable, funny, and sexy as ever."

—*The Rock Stars of Romance*

"Witty dialogue, a quirky and lovable cast, and a whirlwind of a romance. . . ."

—*Peace Love Books*

"A great summer read, fantastic for lazing about and having fun with."

—*Under the Covers Book Blog*

"A story that is sure to please."

—*The Reading Café*

"I fell in wholehearted book-love! Fantastic voice, amazing characters!"

—*Teacups and Book Love*

"An entertaining romantic story overflowing with hilarity, passion, and emotion."

—*Sensual Reads*

WALLBANGER

"Sultry, seXXXy, super-awesome . . . we LOVE it!"

—*Perez Hilton*

"An instant classic, with plenty of laugh-out-loud moments and riveting characters."

—Jennifer Probst,
New York Times bestselling author of *Searching for Perfect*

"Fun and frothy, with a bawdy undercurrent and a hero guaranteed to make your knees wobbly. . . . The perfect blend of sex, romance, and baked goods."

—Ruthie Knox,
bestselling author of *About Last Night*

"Alice Clayton strikes again, seducing me with her real-woman sex appeal, unparalleled wit, and addicting snark; leaving me laughing, blushing, and craving knock-all-the-paintings-off-the-wall sex of my very own."

—Humor blogger Brittany Gibbons

"From the brilliantly fun characters to the hilarious, sexy, heartwarming storyline, *Wallbanger* is one that shouldn't be missed. I laughed. I sighed. Mostly, I grinned like an idiot."

—*Tangled Up in Books*

"Finally a woman who knows her way around a man and a KitchenAid Mixer. She had us at zucchini bread!"

—*Curvy Girl Guide*

"A funny, madcap, smexy romantic contemporary. . . . Fast pacing and a smooth-flowing storyline will keep you in stitches. . . ."

—*Smexy Books*

And for her acclaimed Redhead series

"Zany and smoking-hot romance [that] will keep readers in stitches. . . ."

—*RT Book Reviews*

"I adore Grace and Jack. They have such amazing chemistry. The love that flows between them scorches the pages."

—*Smexy Books*

"Steamy romance, witty characters, and a barrel full of laughs. . . ."

—*The Book Vixen*

"Laugh-out-loud funny."

—*Smokin Hot Books*

also by alice clayton

The Redhead Series

The Unidentified Redhead

The Redhead Revealed

The Redhead Plays Her Hand

The Cocktail Series

Wallbanger

Rusty Nailed

Screwdrivered

Mai Tai'd Up

LAST CALL

alice clayton

G

GALLERY BOOKS

NEW YORK   LONDON   TORONTO   SYDNEY   NEW DELHI

G

Gallery Books
A Division of Simon & Schuster, Inc.
1230 Avenue of the Americas
New York, NY 10020

First Gallery Books trade paperback edition January 2015

GALLERY BOOKS and colophon are registered trademarks of Simon & Schuster, Inc.

For information about special discounts for bulk purchases, please contact Simon & Schuster Special Sales at 1-866-506-1949 or business@simonandschuster.com.

The Simon & Schuster Speakers Bureau can bring authors to your live event. For more information or to book an event contact the Simon & Schuster Speakers Bureau at 1-866-248-3049 or visit our website at www.simonspeakers.com.

Cover photography by Claudio Dogar-Marinesco

Manufactured in the United States of America

10   9   8   7   6   5   4   3   2   1

Library of Congress Cataloging-in-Publication Data

Clayton, Alice.
    Last call / Alice Clayton.—First Gallery Books trade paperback edition.
        pages ; cm.—(The cocktail series)
    I. Title.
    PS3603.L3968L37 2015
    813'.6—dc23   2014040156

ISBN 978-1-4767-6676-8
ISBN 978-1-4767-6677-5 (ebook)

This book is dedicated to Edward Cullen.
Because . . . Edward Cullen.

acknowledgments

The story of Simon and Caroline began somewhere back in 2009. I was a part of this wonderful community of writers and readers and reviewers and all around crazy-town sillies called Twilight Fan Fiction. Some of you readers have been around since then; some came on board well after I had left that particular station. I mention it here because, as I sit at my desk putting the finishing touches on *Last Call*, I know in my heart that it was this very community that put me on the path I'm on today.

I was asked in an interview once which book changed my life. Remember that *Friends* episode when the girls were against the boys in a contest to prove who knew whom best? The question was "What does Rachel say is her favorite movie?" The answer given, *"Dangerous Liaisons."* A follow-up question: "What is her *actual* favorite movie?" *"Weekend at Bernie's."*

So, Alice Clayton. Which book changed your life?

Officially, I felt as though I should answer something very meaningful and smartypants. Something that would illuminate my inner spirit and show me to be some kind of incredibly enlightened literati. But the truth is, *Twilight* is a great fucking book. And it really did change my life. If the question had been "What's your favorite book?" it would be *The Stand* by Stephen King. Love it. Reread it every single year. But it didn't change my life, and *Twilight*, oddly enough, did.

When I found this fan-fiction community, it let me get my fix of Edward, sure. But it also opened my eyes to the idea that *I* might be able to tell a story. Build my own world, tell some silly tales, indulge my inner dirty birdie. And I had a blast doing it. I met people who have become my very best friends. But what it really did, in a much broader context, was allow me to tap into a creative side of my brain that had been silenced for years. It encouraged me to let my silly out, let my crazy flow, and let me rediscover Insane Alice. And it's been the best time of my entire life.

Wallbanger has been translated and published in countries around the world. I'm headed overseas in a few weeks, and I'm lucky enough to be signing books in Prague, people—in F'ING PRAGUE! A city I have been dreaming of visiting since I can remember. And I've just started work on a brand-new series, more of that silly/steamy, funny/smexy stuff that I just can't get out of my head. Stay tuned, chickens; we're going to some new naked places. And I can't wait.

So now I sit, tying up the last little bit of this story, one that began so long ago in chat rooms and blinkie banners. And I'm a little sad. I'm a lot grateful. And I'm intensely excited for the next chapter of this extraordinary life I'm now living.

And it all started with a teenage girl in a hoodie and a 107-year-old virgin vampire.

Thanks.
Alice
xoxo

prologue

A starry night.

A lady in white.

A shoe full of fright.

This is the beginning of the end of this love story. Where girls are beautiful and boys are handsome and cats are rock stars. Where friendships endure and relationships mature. Skirts are flippy and emotions are trippy and everyone gets a happy ending . . . don't they?

Zoom in on happy couples. Zoom in on love everlasting. Zoom in on a chapel.

This is the way the story ends.

This is the way the story ends.

This is the way the story ends.

Not with a whimper, but with a bang.

chapter one

"This is bad. This is *so* bad."

"It's okay, we can . . . wow, it really got everywhere, didn't it?" I said.

"This is bad. This is so bad," Sophia repeated.

"Just get me some paper towels, I can try and wash this off . . . Christ, that's disgusting."

"This is bad. This is *so* bad."

I stomped my feet in protest. "Will you stop saying that? We have to fix this before—shit."

Mimi had just arrived.

"What the *hell* is on my wedding dress?"

The fastest way to get demoted from bridesmaid to dishonored guest is to vomit on the bride's wedding gown. But if you do ever vomit on a wedding gown, make sure the bride is the perfect mix of anal-retentive, hyper planner, and fairy-tale whimsical.

Mimi was a type A personality with a side of Disney.

Which meant she couldn't decide on one wedding gown, so she had two. Custom made. One for the ceremony, one for the reception. So when one was defiled by semi-digested corn flakes, and I mean defiled, she went into crisis-averting mode and immediately pronounced herself a genius for having the foresight to purchase two gowns. Reception gown became main event gown, and all was peaceful in the land of tulle and lace.

Until we realized that there were also semidigested corn flakes splattered across her Jimmy Choo bridal shoes. And maybe a flake or two *inside* as well . . .

In the end, it was Sophia's belly that saved her from being banished from the church. I held Mimi back, but barely. She was strong for only being ninety-eight pounds.

"You ruined my Choos!"

"I didn't mean to! You know I can't help it. I'm like a fountain anymore, it just comes spewing out. I'm too hot, I throw up. I'm too cold, I throw up. I get a whiff of perfume—which smells lovely by the way, great choice—I throw up. You should see how many ties of Neil's I've ruined. It's disgusting." She clutched her rounded belly. "But I'm pregnant. You wouldn't hold the miracle of life against me now, would you?"

"Oh boy," I muttered, rolling my eyes. Sophia made the most stunning pregnant woman ever created. We were all in agreement on this. Her skin glowed, her hair was luxurious, her eyes sparkled, and her tits were even more fantastic. Stunning. Except for five or six times a day when her skin would turn green, her forehead would speckle with perspiration, and she'd projectile vomit the entire contents of her stomach everywhere if she couldn't make it to a bathroom in time. Or a garbage can. Or a potted plant. Or the gutter outside her apartment—I was present for that one. But within moments, she'd return to her perfect, shining example of premotherhood, complete with delicate hands placed gently on her bump of baby. Left hand arranged over right, not an accident. She took every opportunity to show off her new engagement ring. As well she should; it was incredible. Rumor has it Neil needed a crane to lift it and get it on her finger . . .

She had currently assumed this defensive position, complete with wide eyes and innocent expression, and blingy bling, as I wrestled with the bride, who was envisioning her carefully orchestrated wedding crashing down around her ears. Which were flaming red; she was really steamed.

"Backup dress, I have. Backup Choos? I don't! What the hell am I going to wear on my feet?"

"Can we clean them?" I asked, tugging her back as she lunged once more at Sophia. Who was currently auditioning to play the part of Mary, before they got to the inn.

"They're not going to be clean in time! Besides, I'm not walking around on my wedding day with feet that smell like stomach lining!" Mimi cried.

"Okay, now I'm getting a little nauseous. Can we

stop all the vomit talk?" I asked, swallowing thickly. "You can wear my shoes; I'll go barefoot."

"You have giant Anglo feet! I'd be flopping around like a clown all day in those gunboats!" Mimi shouted.

By the way? I only wear a size seven.

"I can't wear anyone else's shoes unless you can find someone with size-five feet and exquisite taste in twenty minutes!" Her lower lip started to tremble.

I looked frantically at Sophia, who I knew already felt terrible about what she'd done. As I was mentally calculating how fast I could get to the closest high-end department store, there was a knock on the door.

"Mimi?" Ryan's voice. "Mimi, you in there?"

"Ryan? Ryan, you can't be here, you can't see me!" Mimi freed herself from my arms and ran to hide behind the door, clad only in white satin panties, a white lace corset, and a blue ribboned garter. Had I forgotten to mention that? "Seriously, it's bad luck to see the bride before the—"

"Hush, you silly girl. I'd never mess with tradition like that," he soothed. "I just wanted to tell you something—you know, before the whole walk-down-the-aisle thing."

"Oh?" she asked, leaning against the door.

"Yeah. I just wanted to say . . . well, I'm so lucky. I'm the luckiest guy I know, getting to marry the girl of my dreams."

"Oh," she whispered, pressing her hand against the wood.

"Ohhh," Sophia and I mouthed to each other, linking arms and listening.

"And I can't wait to marry you—like, I literally can't wait. I know it's happening in an hour, but it's too long, you know?"

"I know," she sighed, and relaxed against the door. Gown? Forgotten. Choos? Forgotten. "I love you so much."

"I love you too, sweet girl," he whispered, and Sophia and I sighed together. "I also can't wait for our honeymoon. I'm going to throw you down on that bed and peel that dress off of you as fast as I can. I can't wait to fuck my wife."

"Uh, sweetie? The girls are in here."

"Shit."

"Hi, Ryan," Sophia and I said, once more in unison.

"Shit," he said again.

"But, wow, does that sound good," Mimi said softly.

Ryan chuckled on the other side of the door. "Okay, I'll let you get back to your bride stuff. I just, wanted to tell you that."

"See you in there," Mimi smiled, and we could hear him walking away. She turned back to us, her eyes bright. "I'm going to marry that man barefoot. Because who the hell cares."

She ran at us, a tiny, happy torpedo, and hugged us both tight. And just like that, Sophia was back in the wedding party.

• • •

Crisis averted, the wedding went off without a hitch. No more vomit, lots of laughter, and lots of tears. And one pair of perfectly pedicured feet dancing down the aisle toward the groom. Mimi's gown was tea length, sculptured satin crafted on a 1950s pattern. The fact that she was barefoot? Charming. Her smile? Evident from outer space. Matched only by the one on her husband-to-be's face as he watched her approach.

The ceremony was brief by Roman Catholic standards, and beautiful. And speaking of beautiful . . .

I would never get tired of looking at Simon Parker in a tuxedo. Especially at the end of an aisle. Not going to lie, it gave me thoughts. Especially when during the ceremony he caught my eye more than once. Sometimes we simply grinned, enjoying the moment with our friends. Sometimes he looked thoughtful, as weddings tend to make everyone think about the future and the past. And once, those sapphire eyes burned into mine, hinting at what he'd rather be doing than standing at an altar. And what he'd rather be doing was me.

In case that was in any way unclear.

As the happy couple made their way down the aisle to applause and well-wishers, Neil followed with his very pregnant girlfriend, Sophia. Then Simon stepped down the few altar steps, slipped my hand into his arm, and walked me down the aisle as well. "Beautiful."

"It *was* a beautiful ceremony."

"Wasn't talking about the ceremony," he whispered,

his gaze dropping down my body, down past the rus-
set silk, the palest tea-colored shantung, the perfectly
dyed peep-toe pumps, and back up again to settle on my
cleavage. Amply displayed. Mimi liked a low-cut dress
on her ladies in waiting.

"That's very sweet."

"Those are very sweet," he murmured, still gazing
at the girls.

"Eyes up here, Mr. Parker," I instructed, squeezing
his forearm. And as I did, I was reminded once more
of the innate strength of this man—my man. Long and
lean, tall and impossibly good looking with his dark hair
and his blue eyes, and his powerful hands holding me
steady as he thrust into me from . . . wait. What?

"Where'd you just go?" he asked, his eyes curious.

"Someplace naughty," I teased, a blush warming my
cheeks.

Sweeping a piece of my blond hair back behind my
ear, he leaned closer and dropped a kiss on my neck,
just below my ear.

"I knew I should have changed your name from
Nightie Girl to Naughty Girl."

"Quiet, Wallbanger; we've got a receiving line to get
through. Then pictures. Then cocktail hour. Then dinner. Then dancing. We'll be lucky to *have* any naughty
times before tomorrow."

"Quickie in the coatroom?"

"Nope, that concept was ruined for me by those
two." I laughed, pointing at Sophia and Neil.

His hand was firmly on Sophia's bottom, church be damned. Since announcing their pregnancy a few months ago, Sophia had put on about thirty pounds, and they all went to her boobs and her butt. Neil could literally not get enough.

"Doggie style. All day. All night. That's all he wants. He can't stop looking at it, touching it, kissing it, rubbing it. It's like I'm just one giant ass, there for his enjoyment," Sophia had told Mimi and me one day at lunch, to the immense pleasure of our waiter, who was hovering extremely close that day. My water glass never dipped below two-thirds full.

Simon leaned in once more, just before we got to the end of the pews. "What if I told you I know a place perfectly suited for a quickie, guaranteed no one will find out?" His breath warmed my skin, and some other parts.

"You're like the devil," I whispered back, shivering deliciously.

"Caroline. Please. We're in church," he chided with a twinkle in his eye. Ungh. *Loved* this guy.

We had now reached the front steps. And as we all spilled out onto the sidewalk below, we watched Ryan swing his new bride around in a circle, her feet kicked up in the air, arms tight around his neck as she laughed and laughed. The crowd oohed and aahed appropriately, and my friends and I gathered to watch and smile as the first of our crew made it official.

"How long are you going to make Neil wait until he gets to be the one swinging you around like that?" I asked Sophia, who stood in front of her baby daddy.

"Six months, post baby. That should be enough time to get this weight off and make sure I look positively killer in my wedding dress," she answered, not-so-subtly rubbing her bum back and forth a bit against Neil. Who groaned and started not-so-subtly thrusting against her backside.

"Whoa, whoa! Can't. Unsee." I shielded my eyes.

"Can't help it. Have you seen her ass? Sweetie, turn around and show them your ass," Neil encouraged, as Simon laughed, clapping him on the back and steering him away from the group.

"I'm gonna take Ass Man here over to congratulate the new Mr. Mimi. You two stay out of trouble," Simon said with a chuckle. And as they walked away, Sophia and I watched them go.

"Speaking of great asses . . ." Sophia said.

"No kidding. And good lord, is it me, or are they both insanely good-looking in their tuxedos?"

"Sort of makes you wonder, doesn't it?" Sophia mused, watching her perfect Ass Man now swing Ryan around in a perfect re-creation.

"Wonder what? When to get married? When we should all make it official? When we all become Mrs. So-and-So?" I asked, my heart leaping into my throat at the idea of becoming Mrs. Parker.

"No." She shook her head, looking at me with a funny expression. "Wonder if Neil's wearing boxer shorts under those tight pants. I don't see a line at all."

"Ah. Well. That's something entirely different," I replied, letting out a little chuckle.

She put her arm around me and squeezed. "Caroline Reynolds, look at you blush."

"Be quiet."

"All excited about the prospect of getting married, making Simon your mister?"

"You think because you're pregnant I won't stomp on your foot?"

"Come on, let's go congratulate our friend Shoeless Joe over there," she said with a smirk, pointing at Mimi, who was surrounded by family and positively beaming.

Ninety minutes later we were drinking champagne under one of the most iconic San Francisco monuments, the Palace of Fine Arts. Mimi had consulted the sun charts, not in an astrological way, but in a perfectly backlit way. So not only was the sun streaming in through the church windows to exactly highlight her skin tone, she had also designed her reception around sunset, capturing that perfect moment when the sun was setting behind the rotunda. And as the lights came on and the candles glowed, the gorgeous old landmark was reflected perfectly in the pond below. Shades of burnished gold from the structure, deep indigo from the water, buttery yellows from the candlelight, and the kaleidoscope of magenta, orange, and fuchsia from the setting sun painted the backdrop of this lovely evening.

It was perfection, as only a professional organizer could ensure. Simon and I mingled with the guests, sipping our bubbly and chatting with strangers, acquaintances, and finally, friends. Up for the wedding after becoming friends with Mimi during her renovation in Mendocino, Viv Franklin was in the house. With her very dashing fiancé, Clark Barrow.

"I can't believe you're pregnant again. William isn't even six months old!" I exclaimed as she told me the news.

"I know, I know! But Clark's got, like, superman sperm or something. I can't explain it. I just enjoy it."

"Vivian!" Clark admonished, his cheeks turning pink as he shook his head at her. "One can share news without sharing everything."

"One can share anything she likes, when she's the one with bun in her very pretty oven," Viv quipped, patting her just-beginning-to show tummy, and effectively shutting down the conversation as Clark now blushed even deeper.

Simon and I had gone up to visit them after the birth of their son, a beautiful little boy. The new parents were ecstatic at their good fortune. They'd been planning their own wedding to be a few months after he was born, but it looked like those plans were on hold for now.

"I want to get married back home, where all my brothers got married," Viv said. "You remember St. Gabriel, don't you, Simon?"

"The church on Seventh Street, right?" he asked. They'd grown up together back east in Pennsylvania.

"That's the one, marrying Franklins off left and right. But Catholics are funny about sin. They'll forgive anything, but they don't like to see it right in their face, know what I mean? My mother would die a thousand deaths if she had a pregnant daughter walking down the aisle," she said with a laugh.

"So we'll wait until after this one is born, and get married sometime next year," Clark finished, wrapping an arm around Viv's shoulders and pulling her in close. "Our own kids will be there when we get hitched. How great is that?"

"Pretty great," Viv agreed, and grinned up at him. Then she turned to me. "And speaking of pretty great, you should see the last few paintings I did. It's a series of how the light changes over the ocean, at different points during the day. They're pretty good, if I do say so myself."

"I'd love to see them. You know I never have any trouble selling your stuff to my clients," I said, thinking of when I might be able to make a trip north. Things were booming at Jillian Designs, and my schedule was full, but not overly so. I had an almost perfect balance now between work and home, and it was pretty freaking great.

I was hired by Jillian after interning here my senior year in college, and she'd become more than a boss, sounding board, and mentor. She'd become a close friend.

In the last year or so, our working relationship had changed. When she first told me she and Benjamin were moving to Amsterdam for six months of each year, I thought my work at her interior design firm was going to change drastically. I'd spent the previous several months running the show while they were on an extended honeymoon, so I was honored when Jillian offered me a partnership. And scared to death. And even more scared to death to turn it down, something most young designers would never do. But my Creative Caroline side had found that the administrative side of running a business wasn't my cuppa. When you're handed the keys to a kingdom, though, you don't walk away.

I didn't walk away, but I didn't snatch the keys either. Jillian and I were able to work out a new arrangement that allowed me to continue to primarily work with clients, and supervise things in a very general sense while she was abroad. We agreed that I'd stay in a mostly creative role, and we brought in a wonderful office manager who helped make sure the lights stayed on and the payroll checks were cut on time.

But things were busy, no mistake. After helping Viv do a renovation on her inherited Victorian home in Mendocino, I'd been retained to work on several restoration jobs around the area, expanding the reach of

Jillian Designs beyond the Bay Area. I'd worked jobs all over Northern California, and as far south as Santa Barbara. I still worked primarily in San Francisco, but the regional work was fun and satisfying. And I was helping to raise the profile of the design firm, which was already fairly well known, even higher.

But as busy as I was, I'd always carve out time for a quick overnight to Mendocino to take a peek at whatever Viv was working on. Sometimes with Simon, sometimes without; it was an easy drive to a lovely location. Viv had converted her attic into a working studio where she started painting the most incredible pieces, all inspired by her recently adopted home of Mendocino. I sold a few to some clients, and word was beginning to spread. Some of her work was featured in a few stores in her area, and she even had a showing at a local art fair here in San Francisco. New pieces? I'd make it work.

"Let me look at my calendar on Monday, see when I might be able to get up there?"

"Sounds good. Simon, how about you coming this time too? We just got two new kayaks," Viv offered, hopeful her adventure partner would come along.

"We'll see. I've got a big trip coming up soon; lots to plan between now and then," Simon said. But I could see his eyes dancing at the thought of kayaking.

"Oh fuck it, you're coming up too, and that's that. Now, I need another root beer. Let's roll, Clark," Viv said, making the decision for him.

"Impossible woman," Clark muttered under his breath, but followed her across the room toward the bar. With a wide grin on his face.

"Those two aren't wasting any time, are they?" Simon said.

"Speaking of not wasting any time . . ." I pointed toward the head table, where Mimi and Ryan were engaging in some pre–wedding night foreplay.

"It's going to be a long night, isn't it?"

"I'll keep you entertained," I murmured, sliding my hand down his back and giving his magnificent buns a quick squeeze.

"Naughty Girl," he said, slipping his hands into my hair and pulling me in for a long, slow kiss. I let him; I didn't care. Surrounded by people at a wedding reception? I kissed him back, his sweet lips opening and his even sweeter tongue tangling with mine. My breath came quickly, my skin heated, and I was ready to take him up on his quickie offer. Until I heard the beginning of the toasts starting over the microphone, signaling it was time for us to return to the head table and be upstanding and proper members of the wedding party.

"Later," he whispered. And promised. Mmm.

The reception went off without a hitch. We all danced, we drank, we danced some more, we definitely drank some more. Sophia and Viv, finally meeting and bonding over their ginger ales, swapped birthing stories and talked endlessly over some kind of sling you carry a baby in.

Whatever it was, they talked about it for hours, it seemed. But since Sophia was the first mommy in our little clan, I was glad she had a new friend who could relate to what she was going through.

By the time we said our good nights to Mimi and Ryan, on their way to spend a night at the Palace Hotel before leaving early the next morning for a honeymoon in Bora Bora, I was pleasantly sauced, and more than pleasantly horny for the man who'd been requesting Glenn Miller all night. But I still found a moment with my girl before she left.

"You were truly the most beautiful bride I've ever seen. Seriously, Mimi, it was an incredible day."

"It was pretty great, wasn't it?" She grinned, lifting up one foot to peer at the sole. "I've got soot foot."

"They're pretty filthy," I agreed. "But you totally pulled it off."

"I know!" She laughed, and fell into a hug.

"Indulging in the fairer sex already?" Sophia asked, appearing out of nowhere.

"Oh c'mere, you," Mimi cried, pulling her into our Mushtown. "You girls are my best friends, you know that?"

"Best friends? Then how come your cousin was your maid of honor?" Sophia teased, and Mimi's face crinkled.

"You know very well it wasn't an option; my mother never would have let me get out of it. I had to have her, and—"

"Tiny. Slow your roll. I was kidding." Sophia laughed, and kissed her on the forehead. "You looked amazing today. Shit, we all did. You threw a great party; congratulations."

"Thank you! And thank you, God, that you didn't fall for Ryan. And thank you, God, for not letting me fall for Neil. I mean, he's super dreamy, and a great kisser, but—"

"Thank God we all ended up with the ones we did. How 'bout we leave it at that?" I interrupted, chuckling as I remembered the weekend at Lake Tahoe when the four of them righted their dating wrongs. What could have ended badly had ended up here. Two of them married, two of them having a baby. We all looked across the dance floor at our three guys. Ties loosened, jackets abandoned, hair messy. Jesus Christ, they were handsome.

"I'm going to get my husband and take him to the honeymoon suite at the Palace," Mimi said with a smile that was equally dreamy . . . and lascivious.

"I'm going to get Simon and let him do things to me in the back of the limo on the way back to Sausalito."

"I'm going to get Neil, a few more pieces of that wedding cake to go, and let him eat me while I eat the cake."

"Oh, for the love of—!"

"Good night, nurse!"

And we sent Mimi off on her honeymoon.

Ninety minutes later . . .

"Simon. Simon. Oh, Jesus, Simon, that's so good, right there, right there, don't stop . . ."

Ninety seconds later . . .

"I can't believe you ate cake while I did that to you."

"Don't worry about it. You can eat cake while I do this to you . . ."

"Caroline, you naughty girl. In the back of a limo— oh, wow, that's good. And this cake is terrific."

chapter two

"So tell me again where we're going? Shopping for pit bulls?" I asked, waiting in the backseat of the Range Rover with Sophia while Simon and Neil stopped for gas. We were headed out of town for the night, spending some time in Sophia's hometown of Monterey. Just a few hours down the coast, it was like a whole new world.

"Yes. Exactly. We're going shopping for pit bulls, Caroline," Sophia replied dryly.

"Well? Aren't we?"

"It's not like shopping for a new handbag. Neil wants a puppy, and so do I. I think it'll be nice to have a puppy and a baby at the same time."

"I think it'd be nuts to have a puppy and a baby at the same time, but hey, I'm just along for the ride," I said. When she showed me her middle finger, I showed her one right back. "Seriously, that's a lot all at once, don't you think?"

"We were planning on getting a dog after the baby, but when my cousin Lucas started texting me these pictures of their latest litter, I just melted. I mean, look at this! Could you resist?" she said, scrolling through her phone and then holding it up to show me six or seven of the tiniest, most adorable puppies, lined up in a row on a pillow, with a proud mama behind them. Some were gray, some were black and white, all of them darling. "And look, video!"

"Oh, God, you're killing me," I sighed, as I watched the puppies wriggling all over the place, jumping and playing and being twelve kinds of cute. "I don't know how I'm going to get Simon out of there without bringing one home."

"Clive would kill you," Sophia replied, shutting off her phone as the boys came back to the car.

"With his bare paws," I agreed.

"Bare paws? Who're we talking about?" Simon asked as he slid behind the wheel.

"Clive. Killing us."

"I have nightmares about that," he replied, shivering. "That cat's way too fucking smart."

"How's his harem doing?" Neil asked.

Simon socked him one on the arm. "Dude. Don't call them that."

"His girlfriends. Sister wives. Whatever. How do you guys not have kittens running all over the place?" Neil asked, rubbing his arm.

"Clive was neutered a long time ago. No nuts for

my boy," I said. "He won those girls over solely with his personality."

When Clive had returned home after his stint as a runaway, he didn't come alone. He'd brought along three lovely lady cats, all of whom adopted Simon and me. We now lived with four, count them, four cats. Norah, Ella, and Dinah now joined Clive in ruling our household, and we just did what we could to get out of the way. Our bed was a bit crowded some nights, but in truth? We wouldn't have it any other way.

"Okay, Neil, let's go over the plan one more time. We pick out one puppy—one—and let's try and go for whichever one seems the calmest. Deal?" Sophia said, reaching up front and putting her hand on his shoulder.

"We'll see," he nodded. His face turned red ten seconds later. Sophia had begun to squeeze, obviously. "One puppy. You got it," he managed, and she gave him a pat on the head. "Cello players. Strongest hands you can imagine. Normally a good thing. But sometimes . . ." he told Simon, who just laughed as we zoomed down the highway, bound for Monterey.

"And this is where we keep all the newer dogs, the ones we haven't worked with as much. Sometimes they can go right in with the other dogs, but they usually need a little doggie detox," the tall blonde said, grinning and making the tour sound fresh, though she'd obviously given it hundreds of times.

We'd made it to Monterey in just under two hours, which was a refreshing change. Whenever Mimi was on a road trip, it always seemed like we had to stop every thirty miles or so for snacks. Once we reached Monterey it was a quick drive up into the hills to Our Gang, a rescue center for abused and abandoned pit bulls. Not knowing much about the breed myself, and only hearing the stories that are usually reported on the news, I didn't know quite what to expect. I certainly didn't expect a former beauty queen to be running the joint. Sophia had filled me in on Chloe, and how she'd gotten the gig, and for someone who'd only been running her own business for just over a year, it was impressive.

"Where are the puppies? I want to see the puppies!" Neil said, practically dancing through the barn we were standing in.

"Easy, Neil, they're just around the corner." Chloe laughed, patting the dog next to her. Sammy Davis Jr. was gentle and sweet, and obviously the mascot of the entire operation. Every volunteer she had working today stopped to say hello to him. Since I had a cat named Clive, who was I to judge what people named their pets?

"So how many people do you have working here?" I asked Chloe as we headed to where I assumed the puppies were.

"Full time there's just three of us, but I have six more part-time paid staff, and usually from seven to ten part-time volunteers, depending on the time of year and where we are in the semester. We've partnered up with a local veterinary college, and there's usually someone interning here for credit. Plus my boyfriend, Lucas. He's a veterinarian here in town, and he's up here all the time."

"You mean my cousin Lucas," Sophia piped up.

"No, I mean my boyfriend, Lucas," Chloe replied, tilting her head and smiling sweetly back at her.

"He's my cousin."

"He's my boyfriend."

"Shit, I like you so much better than his ex!" Sophia exclaimed, just as a very good-looking guy came around the corner.

"You picking on my cousin, Chlo?" he asked, wrapping an arm around her shoulders and pulling her into his side.

"I have to. She's being prickly," Chloe replied promptly, and Sophia stuck out her tongue. "Lucas, this is Simon and Caroline, they're friends of—"

"They're my friends, and I can introduce them," Sophia interrupted. With as much crap as she was giving Chloe, I could tell she really liked her. "This is Simon and Caroline."

"Nice to meet you Caroline, Simon," Lucas said, reaching out and first shaking my hand, and then Simon's. "I hear you guys are picking out a puppy to take back to the city?"

"Oh no, not us. Those two." Simon pointed at Neil and Sophia. "We've got all we can handle with four cats at home."

"Four cats? Wow, impressive," Lucas said as we headed into a separate area. And then we finally saw . . . the puppies. And they were every bit as cute as promised. Neil immediately fell to the floor, letting them crawl all over him in a giant wave of adorable.

"Oh my God! These guys are awesome!" he cried out, now lying down in the pile of waggly tails. They swarmed him, to his delight.

As we watched our friend roll around on the floor, laughing his head off, I had a sudden vision of what Neil would be like as a father.

"You do know that you'll never get to play good cop with your kid, right?" I whispered to Sophia, who just shook her head as she looked on in amusement.

"Oh yeah, that's obvious," she said, then turned to me with a grin. "Besides, I look really good when I'm playing bad cop."

"I'm going to stop you right there," Simon said, then lay down in the pile with his friend.

And as I watched Simon play with the puppies, I had a sudden vision of him rolling around on the floor in our home, in Sausalito, covered in kittens and babies. Mmm, good vision.

"So, obviously they're all adorable," Chloe said, watching the two grown men having a ball with a bunch of dogs. "Any thoughts on which you think you'd like?"

"Good lord, how in the world are we going to choose?" Sophia bent down to pick up a sweet little one that had begun nuzzling at her foot.

Ha! Sophie's choice . . . I bit it back and said nothing. I did look down to see Simon, grinning up at me
with hands full of puppies.

"A hundred percent no," I said, arching my eyebrow.

In the end, it was the puppies who made the choice for
Sophia and Neil. Not one, not two, but three puppies
had been adopted. Cute won out over common sense,
and even Sophia was excited about the prospect of
having a houseful of paws and toddler toes all at once.
Truth was, I'd never seen her happier. She still talked a
great game, tough as nails and seeming to have Neil by
the balls, but she was thrilled with the turn her life was
taking. The puppy trifecta was just one more sign that
our leggy redhead was being domesticated.

We were all racing toward our thirties, settling down
a bit perhaps, but never actually settling.

Lucas and Chloe invited us to stay for dinner. Neil
and Sophia were staying the night. Simon and I had
made reservations at a little boutique hotel down by the
ocean, and I was looking forward to being lulled to sleep
by the sounds of the waves. I was also looking forward
to making Chloe give me a tour of the crazy house she
lived in.

"Seriously, this house is like a time capsule! I've
never seen anything like it—are you sure you didn't get
a designer to re-create 1958 in here?" I gasped, taking
in all the kitsch.

"No way. Everything here is authentic, placed here by my grandparents and untouched for years. Even though it was a vacation home, I'm still amazed how well everything has stood up over the years—it's all still in great shape."

"I could literally sell every piece in this house to my clients; everyone wants midcentury right now. Jesus, is that a hi-fi system?" I asked, pointing to a large console sideboard with the center piece opened up. A turntable in mint condition sparkled from underneath. I'd had one of these refinished a few years back for a client, but this one was a beauty. Danish design, with clean simple lines; when it was closed it looked like a simple dining room buffet table. Everything I'd seen in this house so far was just full of great details like this.

"Oh yeah, we play records on that thing almost every day. Lucas, get that bad boy fired up!" Chloe called out, bringing her boyfriend out from behind the tiki bar.

"Sure thing, chickie baby," he replied, and a moment later the smooth vocal stylings of Mr. Dean Martin were pouring forth. "Now, who wants a cocktail? I've got zombies over here."

Two hours later, I'd learned a few things. One, zombie cocktails are lethal. Don't have more than you can handle, which for me turned out to be two.

We enjoyed dinner on the patio, and after we finished up the great meal Chloe had made we sat around chatting and drinking coffee, trying to combat the effects of the very delicious but very strong cocktails.

"Might want to go a little lighter on the booze next time," Chloe told Lucas. "We've been working our way through this great tiki bar cocktail recipe book, and some are considerably stronger than others," she said to the rest of us.

"Especially when you're the one in charge of the mai tais" Lucas murmured, and I saw a blush creep into Chloe's cheeks. "So, cousin of mine, when are you two tying the knot? I noticed we haven't received an invitation yet."

Sophia patted her belly. "Not sure, but at least six months after the munchkin gets here. I want to get some of this baby weight off first so I can be stunning."

"You'll be stunning regardless," I interjected.

"I mean prebaby-weight stunning. Sorry, I'm shallow. I said it so you don't have to," she said.

"You're not shallow." I laughed.

"You're pretty shallow," Chloe chimed in, with a smirk. Sophia picked up her knife and mimed slitting her throat. "Shallow *and* violent."

"I told you I liked this girl," Sophia said to Lucas, who threw back his head and laughed. "Speaking of weddings," Sophia continued, and my hand froze on its way to pick up my zombie. "When do you two think you're going to be making things official?"

My ears grew warm, my skin prickled, and my lips

began to compose a retort when I saw that she wasn't looking at me, but rather at her cousin Lucas. My lungs deflated and I snatched up my glass, taking a big gulp of zombie. Big gulp of zombie, what a great name for a . . .

But why the hell did I freeze? Why did I care if she was going to ask Simon and me about when we were going to get married? We'd get married when we wanted to. I mean, right?

As I shuffled through this mental Rolodex of panic, I caught his eye from across the table. He'd watched the whole thing, and he knew me well enough to know exactly what I'd been thinking. He grinned, knowing he'd caught me. I rolled my eyes and tried to act casual, paying extraspecial attention to the conversation that had continued during my freeze frame.

"Hold on—so you guys aren't planning on getting married? Ever?" Sophia asked, looking back and forth at Chloe and Lucas.

"Feisty, back off, it's not really your business," Neil said, rubbing her shoulders.

"No, it's cool. We're not planning on getting married—at least not anytime soon. We were both engaged to other people, both went through the whole wedding planning process, we know what that's like. We're pretty happy just as things are," Lucas said, leaning in and kissing Chloe on the cheek.

"It's true, why mess with a good thing?" Chloe agreed, leaning into his kiss. "Granted, we were both engaged to the wrong people, so one day we might decide to tie the knot. But for now? Not for us."

"I don't trust a girl who doesn't want to wear white," Sophia said, and I slapped at her hand.

"I wear plenty of white. Your cousin here has a thing for pinup girls in white lacey corsets," Chloe shot back.

"Too much—"

"Awesome!" Sophia and Neil shouted at the same time.

While the table dissolved into corset talk, I thought about what Chloe had said. If things were good, why change it? That was obviously working for them, and it was working for Simon and me, as well. Hmmm . . .

I stood on the balcony overlooking the ocean, watching the breakers roll in. Starting slow, just outside my field of vision in the black night, each one grew slowly from underneath, swelling to the top and moving relentlessly toward the shore. Finally rearing up, first white around the edges, then throughout as it fell in on itself, crashing onto the rocks and foaming through every crack and crevice. I watched countless waves, following their inevitable path. Each began the same way; each ended the same way. Time after time, unaltered for eons.

Waves couldn't course correct. They couldn't simply decide one day, hey, I think I'll head south toward Mexico, see what's up down there. The only way they were going anywhere other than where they were intended was if there was some major event. Hurricane. Earthquake. El Niño. Otherwise, they were heading for the shore. You could set your clock by the tide. Eventual. Unavoidable. It's what happened.

Deep thoughts. Although it was hard to sit by the ocean and think shallow thoughts, my mind seemed to always go toward the heavy. It would default to melancholy sometimes; why was that?

"Babe, it's freezing out there, aren't you cold?" Simon called from inside.

"It's not too bad, actually. The fresh air feels nice," I called back. His footsteps grew louder as he came to the door and slid the glass all the way back.

"Seriously, freezing."

"Seriously, come warm me up, then," I replied, shaking my bottom at him slightly. Arms were wound around my waist within seconds. He pulled me back against his chest, hands wrapped around my hips, as I snuggled against him. "This feels nice."

"Agreed," he said into my hair, nuzzling my neck. "So what are you thinking about out here all by yourself?"

"Just watching the waves," I said, sliding my hands into his and wrapping them more firmly around my waist.

"You never just watch the waves, Caroline. You're thinking about something."

"I do too just watch the waves. Look how beautiful it is," I said, scanning the horizon left to right. The waves, the beach, the endless stars . . .

"It *is* beautiful," he agreed. "But I know you were thinking about something out here. You were sighing every thirty seconds."

"I was?" I asked, surprised.

"Sure—that's when I know something's on your mind. Your sighs are off the chart when something's up, babe."

"What? Wait, what?" I asked again, turning around in his arms to stare up at him.

"You think I can't tell, after all this time, when you've got something working up there?" he asked, dropping a kiss on my nose. "So out with it: what's got you sighing on a balcony?"

I sighed without thinking, causing a crease to appear on his forehead as he tried not to laugh. I looked at his face and rolled my eyes a little. Just the one roll.

"Okay, yes." I sighed. "And okay, yes, maybe I was thinking some thoughts."

"Care to share?" he asked, and I took the opportunity to press my face into his chest. "Oh, it's like that, is it? No sharing?"

"No no, it's not that. I don't know that I was necessarily thinking anything—just very vague ideas floating around, not even really thoughts yet. Like, thought . . . adjacent."

"Oh boy, we are really going all around this one."

He chuckled. "So let's start with the thought adjacent. What's up, babe?"

"Have you ever watched waves and wondered, what if one wave wanted to go in another direction?"

"Watched waves, yes. Thought about assigning intelligent thought to waves? Nope. Can't say that I have." He looked more closely at me. "But now I'm curious. What thoughts do you think these waves are having?"

"It's not the waves, per se. Just . . . the idea that they have no choice. They have their path, and that's it. All roads lead to the beach."

"What a terrible road," he teased, and I socked him.

"You asked for my thoughts; these are my thoughts. I didn't say they made any sense—they hadn't gotten to that point yet," I said, and he held me closer.

"Nightie Girl, your thoughts make perfect sense, considering the dinner conversation tonight."

"Huh?"

"The panic on your face when you thought someone was asking about us getting married. Now you're out here worrying about waves making different choices. Not that hard a leap to make. It's not like I just met you, you know." I could feel him smiling against my neck, and if it was possible for me to hold him tighter, I wasn't aware of it.

"I wasn't panicked; it just surprised me, is all. And then when it wasn't actually about me, about us . . . I don't know, I just . . . I wasn't prepared to answer that question, I guess."

"What if I were the one asking it?"

"Wait . . . what?" I asked, lifting my chin and looking up at him. In the moonlight, his eyes were the deepest blue, and fixed solidly on me. Studying me, looking for a reaction. "You're not asking me to—"

"No, I'm not asking you to . . . Just asking you how you feel about it, in the general sense. No panic, please."

"I'm not panicking. I'm perfectly calm," I answered, then showed him my best facial tic.

"That's sexy, babe," he said, and laughed.

"You're asking me how I feel about marriage in general, or marriage with someone specific in mind?"

"Either. Or both."

I leaned back to look at him, his hands still on my waist. "I think marriage in the general sense is something I'm in favor of. I also think there's something to be said for the saying 'if it ain't broke, don't fix it.' It seems to be working for Chloe and Lucas. On the other hand," I said, sliding my hands up his arms to link behind his neck, "I think marriage with someone specific in mind is also something I'm in favor of—although it would depend on who the someone specific is, of course. Is there a candidate?"

"Possibly," he answered, beginning to slowly reel me back in closer to his chest. "Very possibly."

"Is he tall? Witty? Charming? Impossibly good looking?" I asked.

"Yes. All of those things." He nodded, looking very serious.

I smothered a laugh, rising on tiptoe to press a very loud kiss just below his ear. "You tell this potential fiancé of mine that if he wants my real answer, he has to ask the real question. Until then, this is all chitchat on a balcony. And I've had enough chitchat for one evening."

"How about sex on a balcony?"

"See, now that sounds more like it." I grinned as his hands slid down my back and around my bottom, pressing me into his hips. As his lips met mine, slow and unhurried, I thought about kissing this specific man for the rest of my life. How could anything possibly be better than this? Simon and me, about to be naked and sexy—could anything top this?

And then I had a vision of this moment happening sometime in the future, but instead of Simon unbuttoning my shirt, he was untying my corset. And instead of sliding my jeans down, he was slipping a blue lacy garter down my thigh. And instead of calling me Nightie Girl as he licked a path from my belly button south, he called me *wife*.

If he was at all surprised by how aggressive I was with him on the balcony, he didn't let on. He simply enjoyed it. Twice. Three times . . .

"But three? Seriously, three?"

"It'll be fun!"

"It'll be chaos! How in the world are you going to manage three puppies, a newborn, and Neil?"

"I'm nesting. I'm hormonal."

"You're psychotic."

"Also a distinct possibility," Sophia admitted as we sat in the back of the Rover on our way back to San Francisco. Simon and I had driven back to Chloe's ranch earlier that morning to say good-bye to her and Lucas and the puppies, and to pick up Sophia and Neil. They'd be heading back down in a month or so, when the puppies were old enough to leave their mother and begin their new city life.

Though I adored the puppies, I thought she was getting in over her head with so much change too quickly. But, as she was fond of telling me, sometimes it was okay to "shut the fuck up and the back the fuck off," and just let them figure it out. But I still told her she was psychotic.

"Speaking of psychotic, I tried to call you last night to tell you *Psycho* was on the late-night movie."

"Oh?" I asked innocently.

"Yeah, I called you like three times in a row."

"Something else was happening, three times in a row," I said, speaking out of the side of my mouth so the boys didn't hear.

"Nice," she said, also out of the side of her mouth, while sliding me a sneaky low-five.

"Yeah, all that marriage talk at the dinner table last night made me a little panicky, which made me go inside my head a little too much. Ended up okay, though. I think Simon might be on the marriage train."

"Oh, you think? Forget the marriage train, come and join me on the obvious train—he's totally going to ask you to marry him," she said, which prompted me to put my hand over her mouth to shut her up.

"Everything okay back there?" Simon called, looking at me in the rearview mirror.

"Totally, how's it going up there?" I asked, singsongy.

"Awesome, Simon's letting me drive the radio!" Neil cried out, turning up Def Leppard to an obscene level.

Which thankfully was loud enough to drown out what Sophia was saying, but was even too loud to continue the conversation. So we did what all adult women do . . . we moved it to the text box.

Way too loud with
that train shit,
preggo . . .

> Oh please, like
> this isn't obvious.

Less obvious than
you yelling about
him proposing.

> You're the one
> who said marriage
> train. I was just
> pointing out the
> obvious fact that
> your mister will

eventually be
making you his
missus. DUH.

Yes, we talked
about it. In a more
concrete way last
night than we have
before. Last night
was the first time
we didn't dance
around it—we kind
of danced right
through it.

That's so exciting!

Yes, it is. But no one
has a ring yet, so
settle the fuck down.

Oh don't make
such a big deal
out of this, of
course he's going
to ask you. He
loves you.

I love him.

Okay, this is
getting trite.

Totally. We should
probably start
talking again;
they're going to
wonder what we're
up to back here.

Are you kidding?
Listen to them
singing. They love
this '80s rocker
bullshit. They're
happy as clams.

We still have to start
talking again.

What should we
talk about?

Doesn't matter,
something random.

Okay.

"Did you know they're talking about expanding the
Vera Wang boutique on Geary?"

I hate you . . .

chapter three

Monday morning found me arranging flowers in my office as usual. Cream roses with the very tips tinged peach and raspberry. Gathered in a spiral in a clear glass vase, surrounded by hydrangea leaves for the green around the stems. Set on the far left of my ebony desk, covered with neat stacks of color-coded manila folders. Each folder represented a different private home, office, or public space, and held cost estimates, value projections, palettes, swatches, clippings, and samples. Each one told a story of a new design, a new life being breathed into a space, either existing or brand new. And today was the day that I'd debrief Jillian, just back from Amsterdam.

She'd begun a small consulting business in Amsterdam, taking on a project here and there for new friends in her and Benjamin's new city, and she seemed to be adapting well to a multinational life.

But she was back in the home office now, and expected to be brought up to speed as soon as she was back. Though she was always in touch through email and conference calls, when she came back home she wanted to sink her teeth into every project she could. We were still finding our way with this new setup, but it was working out really well for us.

It was always great having her back in the office; it never seemed quite the same without her click-clacking around on her high heels. Which I could hear now coming up the stairs, along with a chorus of *welcome backs* and *how are you's* from the rest of the staff.

I stepped out of my office just as she rounded the last bend. Black sleeveless dress, knee-high camel leather boots with an impossibly tall heel, hair tied back in her signature chignon; she was pulled together, gorgeous, and looked well rested. And excited to be back.

"Girl! Get over here!" she squealed, setting down her Chanel bag and sweeping me into a perfumed hug.

"I'm so glad to see you!" I replied, letting myself fall into her embrace.

"I've got presents," she said, ushering me down the hall into her own office, which was cleaned weekly during her absences so it never smelled musty or unused. We couldn't have that.

"You don't have to bring me presents every time you come home, you know," I said as she pulled a few boxes out of her satchel.

"Shut it, but open this," she instructed, setting a

pink box down in front of me, then spun toward her tea set in the corner. "Do we have—"

"Hot water is already in there; I just filled it myself a few minutes ago." I knew that the first thing upon her arrival she'd want to have a cup of tea.

"You're the best."

"I've heard that said. And holy shit, where'd you get these?" I exclaimed, holding up a pair of drop earrings. Set into brushed nickel, there were beads in shades of pink, peach, salmon, coral, fuchsia; all the go-to colors in my favorite palette.

"Saw them in a tiny store in Rome and couldn't resist. I said to Benjamin, 'those are Caroline's colors,' and he insisted we buy them."

"Benjamin has always been a little sweet on me," I teased, referring to the constant state of blush I was always in whenever he was around. It wasn't just me either; Sophia and Mimi shared my not-so-secret-crush on Jillian's husband.

"Just put them on and stop imagining all the different ways you can thank him." She laughed, her eyes sparkling. "I saw all the folders on your desk. Want to bring me up to speed over lunch?"

And just like that, Jillian was back in town. All was right with the world.

We spent most of the afternoon working in a corner booth at our favorite restaurant in Chinatown, getting caught up over our sizzling rice and office gossip. Not much escaped Jillian's eye, even across an ocean. But there was still some scuttlebutt to fill her in on, and as we chitted and chatted, I relaxed more and more.

"So tell me all about the wedding?" she asked, after we'd covered everything office related.

I paused, chopsticks halfway into my mouth. "Thah wady?"

"*The* wedding! Mimi and Ryan!"

I chopsticked, chewed, and nodded. "Oh sure, sure, *that* wedding."

"I was sick to miss it, but we had so much going on at that point with the house in Amsterdam it just wasn't possible for us to get back," she said, stirring her mustard sauce. "But I bet it was perfect, wasn't it? Timed down to the millisecond?"

"What's smaller than a millisecond?" I snorted, digging back into my pot stickers. My pulse was racing. What the hell was up with that?

"Oh, I bet. Did she manage everything the entire day, or did she let go and enjoy?"

"She totally enjoyed. She actually had a great day, even though she had a huge dress snafu at the last minute."

"Oh no, what happened?" Jillian slurped her noodles.

"Sophia's had terrible morning sickness—actually, morning, afternoon, evening, and middle-of-the-night sickness. It hit all of a sudden, and blammo—right onto Mimi's wedding dress."

"You're lying."

"I wish that I was! But you know Mimi—she had a

second dress ready to go for her reception, so she just wore that for both."

"I would have died," Jillian moaned.

"Anyone else would have! But she assumes if celebrities get to have more than one wedding dress, then so should she." I laughed, remembering. "Actually, she was more upset about the shoes—she hadn't planned on a backup pair for those."

"Ah jeez, Sophia didn't—"

"Sophia did! A little flyaway yak landed on Mimi's Choos. She flipped her lid over that one. Until Ryan came to see her; then it all melted away."

Jillian shot me a surprised look. "Wait, Ryan came to see her? Before the wedding? I figured Mimi'd be too superstitious for that."

"Oh, she was. She hid behind the door so he didn't see her. But then, oh my goodness, Jillian, it was the sweetest thing. Ryan said something about how much he couldn't wait to marry her, and how he couldn't wait to call her his wife—and then it was like . . . what are shoes?"

"Aww." Jillian sighed.

"Yeah, thank goodness she was okay going barefoot. Or you know my ass would have been running all over town trying to find her some new shoes." I chuckled.

"She got it," Jillian said, her eyes growing soft.

"She got what?" I asked.

"She realized it wasn't about the wedding; it was about the marriage. Her. Him. Together. She got married barefoot because all she cared about was him. That guy. And throw-up shoes weren't going to stop that from happening."

"Yeah, she did seem a little Zen after that," I said, thinking back to the look on her face. "Also a little horny."

"I remember that," she replied with a dreamy look on her face.

"Officially, I should be saying eww. But it's about Benjamin, so please be free with the details."

"Shush. How are things with you and Simon?"

"Hello, segue," I said, shaking my head.

"Hi, deflection, how are things?" she asked again, chasing a carrot around her plate.

"I'm not deflecting; things are good. Things are very good." I smiled, thinking about balcony sex. And when we got back to our home last night, the hallway sex. And this morning in the shower sex. And—

"I can tell by the look on your face, and the way you're sucking that egg roll, that things are very good," she said, pursing her lips.

"Hey, you asked."

"I did, I really did. So, friends getting married, friends having babies—is that making any bells go off for you?" she asked.

I pointed my pot sticker at her. "Do I have a sign on my back that says Will Work for Wedding? Why is everyone asking me that all the time now?"

"Really? *Everyone* is asking you that?" she repeated, pointing her own pot sticker.

"Okay, not everyone. But it *feels* like that's all anybody is talking about lately. Seriously, it's in the air. It's in the water. It may very well be in this pot sticker."

"It's that time—your friends are all moving into a different phase of their lives. When my friends were all getting married and starting their families, I was too busy to date anyone. My entire life was Jillian Designs. Every wedding I went to for one of my girlfriends, everyone asked me who was I dating, and when was I going to think about getting married. It's like, if one goes over the cliff, we all have to." She sipped her tea, then shrugged. "Sorry, I didn't mean to nudge you toward that cliff."

"You didn't. I guess I'm just realizing lately things are changing. I mean, we're all still ridiculous and childish in our own rights sometimes—so it's hard to imagine now that Sophia and Neil are going to be, like, in charge of a person. A tiny person, but still a person." I leaned my head in my hands, having a hard time narrowing down on what I wanted to say. "It's just weird, I guess, everyone growing up."

"Hey. Growing up and being a grown-up are two very different things. I can't see Neil ever being an actual grown-up. And he's on the news, for pity's sake," Jillian said, laughing.

"Are you glad you put in all the time that you did?"

"What do you mean?"

"Back then, building your business. If you could go back and do it the same way, would you have wanted to get married sooner?"

"Depends."

"On what?"

"On whether I'd met Benjamin sooner. I never wanted to get married until I met him. And we didn't get married for a long time. But I knew it'd happen. Because he was my guy. And luckily, I'd been smart enough to wait for my guy." She smiled at me with a knowing look. "Don't you think Simon's your guy?"

The smile that spread over my face was instant, and broad. "Oh. Simon is most certainly my guy."

"So relax. Enjoy it. Worry about you two, and let your friends do their own thing. Marriage is different things to different people, and not everyone needs it. Some people want the piece of paper, some don't need it. Who's to say which is the right choice? Not me, that's for damn sure."

She finished her tea and signaled for the waiter. "Now, if you want to ask me which choice is correct for Peggy Wimple's sectional in her new theater room, I'd be happy to tell you. Because you got it wrong, little miss protégée." She laughed, slapping down a tear sheet from a project I'd in fact just ordered the sectional for. "Let me show you why I'm the Jillian in Jillian Designs."

And she proceeded to do just that. And when she was finished, I had no choice but to agree with her.

Back home, a few nights later.

"Babe, where'd all the little golf pencils go?"

"No one has ever said that sentence before, Simon."

"You know, the little pencils that came with Scattergories? Where are they?"

"Oh. Right, I think Mimi broke them all at the last game night. You know what a sore loser she is."

We were having everyone over to the house tonight for game night, since Jillian and Benjamin were home from Amsterdam. We knew it would be harder to plan these once the baby came, so we wanted to all get together while we still could.

"Why do we always get stuck hosting this night?" Simon asked, poking his head around the door to the bathroom, where I was trying to get ready.

"Because we have the biggest house now, the best entertaining space. That's why," I said, applying my mascara.

"You look like a fish."

"Huh?"

"When you put mascara on. Your mouth hangs open and you look like a fish waiting for bait, every time I've ever seen you put that stuff on. Why is that?"

"It's the only way to put it on."

"But why?"

"No one knows, Simon; it's just what you do when you put mascara on."

"Like as a rule?"

"Stop talking to me while I look like a fish and let me get pretty, for goodness' sake," I squawked, and he disappeared around the corner. I finished putting on my face, and I *did* actually try to finish my mascara with my mouth closed, but it just wasn't possible. I was reaching for my lip gloss when his head popped back around the doorframe.

"By the way, we've been invited to Philadelphia."

"Where the cheesesteaks live? Whatever it's for, we say yes!"

"Yes to cheesesteaks, or yes to the invite?'

"Wasn't kidding at all when I said whatever it's for, we say yes. But now that you mentioned it, what exactly are we invited to?" I hoped he didn't notice that the drooling had officially begun.

"Trevor, my old friend from high school? You remember his wife, Megan, right?"

"You're kidding, right?"

"Okay?" he said, squinting at me in a curious way.

"Megan was able to get me the single most important item in this entire house."

"She got you that new vibrator?"

"Jesus . . ."

"Oh, the cookbook, right," he said, remembering. Megan used to work for the Food Network, and was able to secure me a signed copy of the original *Barefoot Contessa* cookbook. By Ina Garten. Signed to *me* by the way; one of those "Best wishes, Ina" deals. It honest-to-God said:

> *To Caroline—*
> *Best Wishes,*
> *Ina*

Go ahead and be jealous. I'll wait.

Simon, on the other hand, would not.

"Okay, so you remember Megan."

"*Remember* her? Did you not hear me say *single* most important—"

"I got it, babe. Are you at all curious about hearing what they're up to, or are you just going to spend some head-space time dreaming of Ina and her kitchen?"

"And me *in* her kitchen. If you're going to get into my daydream, you have to set the scene correctly. I'm there with Ina, in her kitchen in the Hamptons, and we're cooking up something wonderful for you and her husband, Jeffrey. Something with roasted chicken, which she'll teach me how to carve perfectly. And roasted carrots, which she'll pronounce with that subtle New York accent of hers, where it sounds like she's saying *kerrits*."

"I worry about you sometimes," Simon said, reaching over to feel my forehead.

"I'm perfectly fine. Don't worry about me, I'll continue my fantasy later. So what's up in Philly?"

"Oh, we're back to my story now?" he asked, and I leaned in and kissed him in apology.

"Sorry, babe, tell me all about Trevor and that wonderful wife of his," I said. I was playing with him, but I actually liked both of them. We'd gone back to Simon's hometown for his tenth high school reunion last year, and he was welcomed back like a conquering hero. He hadn't been back since he graduated high school, not long after both of his parents were killed in a car accident. No one had seen him since, and while he was initially nervous about how he'd be received, he was very quickly convinced that everyone was just thrilled he was back. In high school he'd been the homecoming king and everything that you'd assume comes with it. High school Simon was big man on campus. He'd had his own posse of what I called the apostles (his old pals Matthew, Mark, Luke, and John), headed by his old bestie, Trevor. We'd spent a lot of the reunion evening with him and his new wife, Megan, who was then pregnant with their first.

"How are they enjoying their new life with baby?"

"Enough that she's pregnant again," Simon said, and I dropped my lip gloss.

"What the hell is in the water these days? I'm switching to vodka. Always."

"I'll vote yes to that—vodka makes you crazy, and horny. And adventurous. You go on an all-vodka diet, and I'm pretty sure I can convince you to try that thing that you never let me do."

"All the vodka in the world isn't getting you in there, so forget it Simon," I said, poking him with my lip gloss as he pouted. "So, Megan's pregnant again—wow. Tell them congratulations from me."

"That's what started this whole thing. They've invited us out for the christening of baby number one, and to help celebrate baby number two. It's next month; think you can get some time off?"

"For cheesesteaks? I mean for christening? Yes, yes, we should definitely do that." I tried once more for the lip gloss when the doorbell rang. "Great, someone's early. Go ahead and grab some colored pencils out of my bag."

"For what?"

"Scattergories."

"Right!" he exclaimed, then disappeared through the bedroom.

Alone for the moment, I finally applied my lip gloss and allowed myself a thought or two about Megan and Trevor. Two kids, in as many years. Before getting married, Megan had been on the fast track at the Food Network, working in what was in many ways a dream job. But her dream was a family, and she made that happen. And now she was on the baby fast track. Instead of styling artisanal cheese boards and making cream puffs puffier, she was wiping spittle and stepping on baby rattles.

I had a sudden flash image of Simon stepping on a baby rattle that Clive had stolen for his own toy and then left in his path, and I chuckled. Babies babies everywhere, and not a vodka to drink. I finished my lip gloss, twisting the cap shut with a click, and took a deep breath. I chased away rattle thoughts and indulged in a cheesesteak fantasy moment, interrupted by Simon calling out, "Idiots are here!"

Hmmm, that could be anyone—we knew a lot of idiots. Time to go kick some idiot ass in Scattergories . . .

As usual, game night ended in bloodshed. The girls went down, and went down hard. I know exactly how that sounds. But it's true. We sucked a big fat Scattergories dick. And Pictionary dick. And Apples to Apples could very well have been renamed Dicks to Dicks. In the end, the boys won big. But once everyone was gone, and my skirt was up around my ears as Simon took his victory lap . . . ahem . . . all was right with the world.

chapter four

The following broadcast was originally aired on local San Francisco NBC affiliate KNTV . . .

"Hey there, it's Neil coming to you live from Levi's Stadium, where the 49ers are taking on the Seattle Seahawks, their toughest rivals in the NFC West. We'll be with you play-by-play as these two powerhouse teams hash it out on the gridiron. But before the teams take to the field, there's another rivalry playing out, one equally as fiercely competitive as anything inside the stadium. I'm talking, of course, about tailgating. Wieners or bratwurst? Hots or brats? We're going to let these fans put it all on the line, and in the bun, as we taste test the best in tailgating cuisine.

"Now here we have Marcus O'Reilly, a na-

tive of the Bay Area, and a staunch hot dog sup-
porter. He says there's nothing like a good hot
dog at a football game, isn't that right, Marcus?"

"Oh, it sure is, Neil. A hot dog will take out a
bratwurst any day of the week."

"Those are fighting words, Marcus. And I'll
be taking a big bite out of that wiener in just a
moment. Now over here we've got Angus Wheel-
wright, bratwurst enthusiast and, I understand,
an amateur kickboxing champion, is that right?"

"You're right about that, Neil. And I'm here to
say that my bratwurst can kick a hot dog's butt
anywhere, anytime. Bring it, hot dog boy!"

"Whoa, whoa, fellas, let's keep the trash talking on the field, huh? We're just here to enjoy
some delicious sausages before the big game
and . . . Sorry, what's that? I apologize, gentle-
men, I'm getting some breaking news over my
headphone about . . . a baby and a . . . delivery . . . van? Some kind of labor . . . dispute?
Shouldn't we be going back to the studio for this
story? Wait a minute—*who's* in labor? Sophia—
wait, *my* Sophia? I'm on my way, I'm on my way!
John! Gimme the van keys! Gimme the keys so
I can—"

*Audio is dropped at this point as the shot wid-
ens to include two confused sausage enthusiasts,
three confused news crew guys, and an entire le-
gion of tailgating fans eager to be on television, all*

watching as the KNTV satellite van careens away toward the on-ramp, driven by a panicked sportscaster. The last shot we can see before the feed is lost is the newscaster yelling out of the window at drivers to "Pull over, this is a baby emergency" and to "Get out of the way, for God's sake" and "I'm having a baby! Waahooooooo!"

"Are you watching that again?"

"I can't stop. I literally can't stop. It's too fantastic."

"It is pretty great. How many hits is it up to now?" Simon asked.

"Hmm, looks like . . . Jesus Christ, it's over thirty thousand views!" I refreshed the page and watched it climb again.

Neil finding out on air that Sophia had gone into labor had turned into YouTube gold in literally hours. It was posted within minutes of its airing here in the Bay Area, and it was all anyone in town was talking about. Sophia had texted Mimi and me, so we were already en route to the hospital when the on-air incident happened.

Unable to reach Neil, Sophia had contacted his producer, who unwisely began speaking into his ear during his broadcast. Unable to multitask at the best of times, Neil usually received very little feedback during his live segments, as he had trouble concentrating when the "little man in the booth" became the "little man in my ear." But knowing she was in labor, they took a chance and told him.

And the world can now see what happened. His hijacking the affiliate van during the hot dog-versus-bratwurst debate had become comedy gold. Luckily, he was so beloved by viewers that the station had been flooded with emails and calls wishing Neil and Sophia luck in their special delivery.

In the meantime, I was in the hospital waiting room with Simon, Mimi, and Ryan. And I couldn't stop watching the clip.

"He's, like, a legitimate Internet star now," I gushed, refreshing the page once more. "And we're at thirty-*five* thousand views. This is crazy!"

"How many of those came from us?" Ryan asked, watching it on his phone.

"At least a hundred," Mimi answered, watching it on her iPad.

Simon sat down next to me, then stood up and walked over toward the nurses' station, scanned the hallway where our friends were, and then came to sit back down.

"Relax, babe, we'll know something when we're supposed to know something," I told him.

"I know, I know," Simon said, then looked toward the nurses' station again. "How early was she?"

"Only a week, everything's fine," I answered, reaching for his hand and holding it on my lap.

"Oh I know, I know," he said again, squeezing my hand. "I'm gonna go get some coffee, want anything?"

"I'm good, babe, go ahead. Take Ryan."

He nodded, squeezed my hand once more, then he and Ryan headed for the cafeteria. Mimi came and sat down in front of me and leaned against my legs.

"Play with my hair," she commanded, pulling out her ponytail and shaking it out. I ran my fingers through it, separating it for braids. She loved to have her hair braided. "Simon seems worried."

"I think anytime anyone is in the hospital he gets a little jittery. I don't even think he's aware of it," I replied, keeping my eyes on the door where they'd just left. "He'll be fine as soon as we know how Mama's doing."

"It's so crazy. I mean, this morning, Sophia was just Sophia. By tonight? She'll be someone's mother."

"She might already be."

"Shit, you're right," Mimi said, crossing her legs and sitting up straighter. "I always figured I'd be the first with the kiddos."

"So did we." I chuckled, flipping her hair under and over my fingers, weaving it into a plait.

"We're trying, did I tell you that?"

"Shit no! When did that start?"

"Pretty much right after the honeymoon, I stopped taking the pill. We thought we'd wait at first, but we talked about it and we both want a family right away. So we figured, what the hell. Let's do it." She turned back to look at me over her shoulder. "And believe me, we're doing it."

"Atta girl," I said, tugging on her new pigtails.

"I didn't want to say anything until after she had the baby, you know. I didn't want any thunder stealing."

"I don't think you can steal thunder when you don't technically have thunder yet."

"True," she replied, then turned around as the boys came back in.

"Any news yet?" Ryan asked, carrying a tray of coffees. "We grabbed extra, just in case you changed your mind."

"Nothing yet," Mimi answered, springing from the floor to snatch up a coffee. "Come on, let's go look at the babies behind the glass." She led him by the hand as he handed off the tray to Simon.

"How're you doing?" I asked him as he handed me a coffee and sat in the chair next to mine.

"Me? I'm fine, why?" he replied. I looked pointedly at his leg, which was bouncing up and down nervously. "Eh, a little edgy I guess."

"I know." I sighed and leaned my head on his shoulder. We sat in silence for a bit, as silent as a hospital waiting room can ever be.

"I hate hospitals," he said, and I nodded my head against him. "I just hate them. Even good news, like this is obviously going to be, I hate being in them."

"I can imagine," I whispered, and looped my arm through his. He didn't say anything else. And he didn't have to. I sat next to him, and kept my head on his shoulder. A few minutes later, Mimi and Ryan came back in. And a few minutes after that, Neil came walking around the corner from the nurse's station, wearing scrubs and a pie-eating grin.

"You guys want to come meet my daughter?"

Mary Jane: 6.2 pounds, 19¼ inches long. Tiny and pink, with ten perfect fingers and ten perfect toes. And one giant voice. We didn't stay long, since by then both sets of grandparents were swarming. But we stayed long enough to see both Sophia and the baby. Each of us got to take a turn holding her; each got to take a turn hugging Neil, who was Mr. Waterworks. There were many *dude*s said, many backslaps and half hugs exchanged. And when the four of us finally left the new parents, we were exhausted. Not as exhausted as Sophia, but tired nonetheless.

We said good night, or good morning actually, to Ryan and Mimi, and headed back across the bridge to Sausalito. The sky was just beginning to lighten, just a barely lighter gray than the rest of the sky. Simon was pretty quiet, although he'd been so happy at the hospital. He'd held Mary Jane as long as they would let him. He was so gentle and sweet, nervous, sure, but willing to try it. Did my eyes fill a bit? Oh my goodness, yes. Simon? Holding a baby girl? It was like a bomb of cute went off inside me. Still, he was quiet now. Thoughtful.

I pushed the door open first, bracing myself for a rush toward my ankles. First came Norah, our sweet little calico. Always the first to greet, she trotted over and promptly laid on top of my feet, rolling back and forth in delight that her people were home. Only a few seconds later, in strolled Ella, long and lean and beautiful. She headed straight for Simon, as ever. She was a one-woman cat for sure. She tolerated me, but she adored Simon. Thumping down the stairs one at a time came Dinah, meowing and chirping at the top of her lungs, seeming to say "Hello hello, where have you been? Hello hello, why did you leave? Hello hello, why would anyone ever leave here?"

"Hi, sweet girls, how've you been? Did you miss us?" I cooed, scooping up both Norah and Dinah, while Ella languished in Simon's arms like she was born to be placed there. And on the landing, just around the corner, sat Clive. Calmly licking his paws and staring at us all with bland disinterest.

When Clive ran away last year, we had been devastated. He was lost for weeks, and while we had kept up the search, over time I had to admit that the chances of him ever returning were growing slimmer by the day. Until one night when he surprised us both by just waltzing into the backyard and back into our lives. And he wasn't traveling alone. No sir, my boy had been busy squiring half the town. He'd brought home not one girlfriend, but three. And as ridiculous at it seemed at the time, adopting three more cats into our household had proved to be a wonderful idea. Now Clive had his harem, and we had three more personalities to keep us entertained. And entertained we were, on the daily.

"Are you hungry? I can make you something," I offered as we all headed into the kitchen. Clive in tow now as well, winding his way through my ankles in greeting.

"I don't think so," Simon replied, looking out the bay window, still holding Ella.

"Okay, I'm going to go run through the shower real quick then before bed."

"Okay, babe," he said, and before I went upstairs I went to him.

"Love you," I whispered, planting a kiss on his neck.

"Love you," he replied.

I left him standing by the window, thinking his thoughts, whatever they might be. In the time I'd been with Simon, I'd learned that sometimes he just went inside himself a little, needed a moment or two alone when something was particularly emotional. Like today had been. He'd talk when he was ready.

I dragged myself up the stairs, straightening a painting as I went. Living in Northern California, we might not feel *every* earthquake tremor, but I was constantly straightening frames. As I walked into our bedroom, I sighed as I always did at the sight of it. Soft area rugs laid over gorgeous deep-toned wood floors, puddles of linen hanging from the rods over the windows that looked out over the bay and, in the distance, San Francisco. I kicked off my shoes, stripped off my clothes, and headed into the bathroom, where I flipped on the steam shower and let the glass begin to cloud. I yawned as I dragged a brush through my hair, trying to get most of the snarls out before getting it wet. I might have to take a personal day today, stay in bed. I was beat. I could hear Simon walking up the stairs, and I called out to him.

"I'm getting in, babe, if you want to join me. You know, for conservation's sake only. No ulterior motive at all." I laughed silently to myself as I heard his steps quicken, and I slipped in before he got to the bathroom. I stood under the spray, eyes closed, letting the warm water sweep down over my tired muscles. I heard him enter the room, heard the sound of his shoes kicking off, heard the sound of his belt buckle jingling, heard the slide of denim moving down down down and then hitting the floor. I heard the shower door creak open on the other side of the steam and I smiled underneath the spray, raising my hands to my hair and arching backward in a very specific way. I was tired, sure. But I was never too tired for his hands and his mouth and his everything else he had to offer. So I arched. And waited. And arched some more. And still, waited. I peeked out from underneath the water, and he stood there. His eyes poured over my skin, his mouth set . . . and tense.

"Babe?" I asked, leaning forward to wrap my hands

around the back of his neck, just as his hands slipped around my waist, fingers digging into my skin. "You okay?"

Water poured down over both of us, wetting his skin, sliding against mine as the steam created a little puffy cloud of our very own. The shower disappeared, the world disappeared, and in the middle of that world it was just me and my Simon. His lips parted, one stream of water trickling down, wetting his lips and making them irresistible to mine. But before I could bring my mouth to his, he spoke.

"Marry me."

A statement. Not a question. It came again.

"Marry. Me." His eyes burned into mine.

I breathed in, my ears ringing. My pulse sped up, my heart raced, I was trying to remember exactly what breathing meant. I was wet, and I was gasping.

"I want you. I want that, what they had today. I want it all, and I want it with you. I want you, want you to be my wife. I've got a ring, I'll give it to you right now if you'll say yes." With every word, his hands tightened on my hips, desperate, crazy, longing. "I had this all planned out, so much smoother and romantic and everything you deserve. But my head's been spinning since yesterday, when I saw my best friend steal a van to go meet his new family. And all I want, all I've ever wanted, is exactly that. Exactly you. And when I walked up those stairs, and heard the shower go on, and knew you were in here all naked and wet and waiting for me, I knew I couldn't wait another day, another hour, another minute, without asking you to be my wife. So. Marry. Me."

He knelt. Christ on a crutch, he knelt on the shower floor, where he had knelt countless times before . . . ahem . . . took my hand, and repeated those words again. Finally, with a question mark at the end.

"Marry me?"

And in that moment, I realized all the worrying, all the hand wringing and wonder ponder, all the thoughts about who says what's right for a couple, and when is it too soon, and when is it the right time, and if it ain't broke don't blah blah blah. Fuck all that noise. It wasn't about what was right for other couples, it was about what was right for us. Simon and me. Because when Wallbanger kneels down and asks you to be his wife, it's not really something you need to think too long on.

Funny thing about getting proposed to in a shower. You can't tell which is water and which is tears.

I said yes, and then he kissed me. I said yes, and then he touched me. I said yes, and then he slipped inside me. I said yes, yes, yes, and then he loved me.

Sometime later, he carried me to our bed, took a ring from his bedside table, and slid it onto the fourth finger of my left hand. It was shiny and sparkly and perfect and beautiful and looked amazing when I was clutching his backside as he pressed into me again.

"I can't believe . . . you asked me . . . to marry you . . ." I panted as he thrust hard.

"Believe it, babe," he murmured, rolling us both so that I was perched on top of him.

"I can't believe . . . how lucky . . . I am . . ." I panted once more, getting into my rhythm.

"Wrong." He sat up underneath me, driving deeper into my body. "I'm the lucky one." I gasped, he groaned, and my hips went wild.

"I can't believe . . . you're going to be . . . Simon . . . Reynolds . . ."

Yeah, I got rolled over for that one.

I made my fiancé scrambled eggs for breakfast. Can you believe that? Not the scrambled eggs part, although they were pretty unbelievable. Old Barefoot Contessa trick. Beat the eggs with a few tablespoons of cream, then gently pour into a buttered pan, stirring lightly over low heat. Perfect eggs, every time. À la Ina. À la sparkly ring. À la 2.5 carat cushion cut on a platinum band. I couldn't stop looking at it. I added some kosher salt to the eggs. I marveled at my ring in front of the salt box, noting how nice it looked next to the Morton's girl. I added a twist or two of freshly ground cracked pepper. I gazed at how my ring caught the light and made tiny rainbows on the countertop.

I opened every single cabinet and every single drawer in that kitchen, just to see how my ring looked against each panel. This was normal behavior, I mean, right?

"I can't stop looking at my ring," I confided to Simon

as I set a plate in front of him along with a glass of freshly squeezed orange juice. The juice was freshly squeezed because I wanted to see how my ring looked while my hands were . . . turning on the juicer.

"I can't stop looking at it either," he admitted, pulling me onto his lap for a hug.

"That's sweet, babe."

"Of course, I'm usually looking at your tits, so this ring stuff is kind of cutting into that time."

"That's weird, babe."

"Have you told anyone yet?"

"Hasn't really been time. I've been too busy fucking my fiancé since it happened."

"That's literally the sexiest thing you've ever said to me."

"Really? How about the time I told you to lick my sweet—"

The great thing about scrambled eggs is they're so easy to make again when the first batch gets too cold to eat.

Moments later, as we lay on the kitchen table, we heard the sound of a plate crashing to the floor.

"You owe me for that plate," I said.

"You owe me for that orgasm."

There was another crash. "Oops. Sorry about that," I said, not at all sorry.

"When I broke your plate it was accidental, in a fit of passion. Pushing plates off the table on purpose isn't going to get you anywhere, Caroline."

"I doubt that, Simon. Look how fantastic this ring looks on my hand while it's holding your cock."

"Jesus Christ, woman."

Moments later . . .

"I heard you on the phone with Jillian earlier. You really didn't tell her?"

"No, I told her I was taking a personal day but I didn't say why."

"Why are you taking a personal day?"

"To fuck your brains out underneath our kitchen table."

"I see."

"You have a problem with this?"

"It's the best use of a personal day I can think of."

"Agreed. Now, let's get to it."

"Are you going to be this bossy when we're married?"

"You have no idea, Simon. You have no idea."

Hours later . . .

"I'm seriously hungry."

"Me too. Can you control yourself?"

"Me? You're the one that was pushing plates off the table on purpose."

"Don't start that again. Let's grab something on the way to the hospital."

"Are you having a heart attack? I know that last round was pretty intense. Thanks for being so bendy, by the way."

"You're welcome, and no on the heart attack business. I told Sophia I'd stop by today, see how she and the little one are doing."

"So we have to put on clothes now, I suppose."

"If you want to make it past security, it's a safe bet. Come on, I want to call my mom and tell her the good news."

"What about your dad?"

"You get to call him, and explain why you didn't talk to him first before asking me to be your lawfully wedded wifey."

"Shit. I mean, yay."

Simon and I called my parents, who were ecstatic. My mom immediately shifted into wedding mode, asking me all kinds of questions about when and where and had I thought about colors and did I want my cousin Bernice to be a bridesmaid and made me tell her every detail about when he asked me to marry him. I left out the detail about us being naked at the time; that part was for me and me alone. I knew girls who'd been asked in a horse-drawn carriage, on the beach, at the top of the Eiffel Tower, even on the BART. But no one I knew had a naked engagement moment. Oh sure, afterward I assumed most were naked. But during the actual moment? I wanted to keep that to myself.

We got dressed, finally, piled into the car, and headed back into the city after stopping for cheeseburgers and milkshakes. Did I show my ring to every person working the drive-thru that day? You bet your sweet bippy I did. Here's me and my ring biting into a burger; here's me and my ring drinking a milkshake. I even had Simon re-create the moment by sliding an onion ring down my finger. For someone who'd originally questioned the entire idea of getting married and whether it was necessary, I was sure turned around by a sparkly something.

When we got to the hospital, I turned the ring around, facing the diamond into the palm of my hand. I didn't want Sophia to see it right away. I knew what Mimi was saying about the thunder stealing. I knew she'd be happy for me, but this was still very much about little Mary Jane, and I wanted to make sure we saw her first.

We knocked, and Sophia gave us the go-ahead to come in. Sitting up in her bed, makeup flawless and hair shining, she was eating take-out fried chicken while Neil sprawled on the couch, holding Mary Jane close to his chest.

"Hi!" Sophia called out, pausing from her chicken frenzy for only a moment to say hello. "Sorry, I'm starving and this hospital food was just not cutting it. I just pushed a baby out of my coochie, and all they want to give me is Jell-O? Fuck that, I needed something real."

Every thought I'd had about Sophia softening into motherhood went right out the window. Thank goodness.

Mary Jane let out the tiniest gurgle and coo, and four pairs of eyes locked on the bundle in Neil's arms. Sophia beamed. Okay, she'd softened a bit.

"How're you feeling, Mama?" I asked, crossing over to her and smoothing her hair back. "You look fantastic."

"I do, I really do. You should have seen me this morning though, I looked dreadful. Now I know why the Kardashians have the glam squad stop by after every birth; otherwise you look half dead in every picture with your newborn."

"You look gorgeous," Neil insisted. "Before or after any glam squad."

Sophia beamed again. Simon had sat down next to Neil on the couch, and was examining the pink bundle.

"Dude, you can totally hold her, just ask." Neil puffed out his chest, causing the bundle to rise up and out.

"I guess I could, just for a minute," Simon replied, stealing a quick look at me. I grinned back, grateful to get another chance to watch Simon holding a baby. Hello, ovaries, I wondered when you were going to sit up straight.

Sophia and I watched the two guys transfer Mary Jane between them with all the precision of a tactical nuke team disarming a warhead. It took all I could not to giggle out loud, but it was incredibly sweet. "So how are you feeling? Like, for real how are you feeling?" I asked Sophia, once the transfer was complete.

"Like I just pushed a baby out of my coochie," she

groaned, biting back into her chicken. "It hurt like a motherfucker. But totally worth it. Have you seen how freaking cute she is?"

"Pretty freaking cute I'd say," I replied. "You up for some more good news?"

"Always," she said through a mouthful. I turned the ring around. She screeched, showing me her chicken and waking her child.

"Soph! What the hell?" Neil cried out as he and Simon both looked at each other and then at Mary Jane when she started crying.

"Let me see that ring!" Sophia yelled.

"Why is she crying?" Simon asked, panicked.

"Her mother scared her half to death!" Neil yelled, also frantic.

"Everyone calm down," I soothed, trying to move over toward the couch, but unable to do so because Sophia had a vicelike grip on my hand. I expected her to pull a jeweler's loupe out of her nightgown.

"How do we make her stop?"

"Just walk her, Simon!"

"I don't know how to stand up with her!"

"Is this two-point-five karats?"

"Call the nurse, she won't stop crying!"

"Babies cry, Neil."

"Someone help us!"

"Go get my baby from the Keystone Cops, would you?"

"Oh, for pity's sake," I said, snatching my hand away

and crossing to the couch. "Hey, little miss, it's okay," I soothed, plucking Mary Jane neatly from Simon's arms and cuddling her close. "Shh, shh, it's okay. No more screaming, I promise. Everyone your parents know just happens to be crazy, okay? Shh, shh . . ." I brought her to Sophia, who began to lower the front of her gown.

"Oh, I, uh . . . I should step out, I, uh . . ." Simon said, getting up from the couch.

"They're just boobs, Simon," Sophia scolded, reaching up for Mary Jane and bringing her to her breast. It was surprising just how natural it all was. Here we all were, four best friends, one of whom had her tits out. And this was just how it was now. Except for Simon's eyeballs, which were currently staring everywhere but where the action was.

Neil came over to stand by the bed, and he finally saw what Sophia had been screaming about.

"Hey, what's that on your finger there?" he asked, looking down at my ring.

"What does it look like?" I teased, holding it up for him to see. He looked back and forth between me, the ring, and finally Simon.

"Dude?"

"Dude."

"Dude!" Neil exclaimed, and picked Simon up off the couch in a giant bear hug. Which he was still doing when Mimi and Ryan peeked around the corner like a totem pole.

"We came to see Mary Jane and bring presents—

what the hell is going on?" Mimi asked, staring at this weird tableau.

"Ask the bride," Sophia said, nodding toward me.

Turns out they frown on screeching in the maternity ward. We were asked, very politely, to leave.

Once more, I found myself in a hospital waiting room with Mimi, Ryan, and Simon, although this time it was a very different subject from the night before.

"I can't believe you're engaged! This is so perfect. I was just beginning to feel my wedding planning blues. I had nothing new to plan! Now I can get started on yours! First things first, have you set a date? Do you know the venue? Evening? Afternoon? Black tie? White tie? I—"

"Slow your roll there, peanut," I cautioned, holding up my hands in the international sigh for stop it, stop it now. "We have literally nothing planned, this whole thing isn't even a day old. We haven't planned a thing, and likely won't just yet," I said, taking a deep breath. "Seriously. Settle."

"Settle. I'll give you settle," Mimi said under her breath, shaking her head. "Okay, but, can I just ask one tiny thing?"

"One."

"What do you think your colors are going to be?" she burst forth, excitement coming off of her in waves.

"Oh boy. I'm going to send you to my mother's, and you two can plan yourselves into oblivion together," I said, laughing when I saw how excited that made her.

"Best idea ever! Oh, Caroline, this is going to be so much fun! I'll call her tonight, see what she's thinking. Oh, there's so much to do, I—"

"Mimi. Sweetie. I was kidding. Just slow down, okay? Let me be engaged for a minute without all this wedding stuff, okay?"

Her face collapsed, but she shut it. For his part, Ryan merely said *dude* a few times, Simon said *dude* a few times, and they clapped each other on the back. Damn them . . .

By the time we got home that night, I had thirteen emails from my mother riddled with suggestions about venues all over Northern California, and seventeen emails from Mimi with links to dresses, shoes, bridesmaids' dresses, and cake vendors. I looked up from the desk in the kitchen where I was going through all of these when Simon came up behind me to rub my shoulders.

"That one's pretty," he said, pointing to a dress on the screen.

"I can't believe these two, Mimi and my mother. They're already starting," I said, shaking my head in disbelief.

"What, taking over?" he asked, chuckling and digging in with his thumbs and making my head roll back with a groan. I gazed up at him.

"Totally. It's going to be a shitshow."

"How can a wedding be a shitshow?"

"I'd let you read these emails, but I think I'm incapable of moving my head right now. Do you know how cute you are when you're upside down?" I murmured, groaning once more as his hands moved down along my arms, hooking around my elbows and bringing them up to rest on his shoulders.

"I like *you* upside down," he murmured right back, leaning down to dust my forehead with the tiniest of kisses.

"How does my ring look upside down?" I teased, holding my hand out in front of me to gaze at it once more.

"Sexy." Kiss. "Impossibly sexy." Kiss. Kiss. "Ludicrously sexy." Kiss. Grope. Grope.

"Ludicrously sexy?" I asked, my eyes fluttering shut as his fingertips danced inside the edge of my bra.

"It's a word."

"So is howfastcanyoubenotsodressed?"

"That's . . . let's see . . . one, two, three—"

"You're counting?"

"—four, five—"

"Simon?"

"Hmm?"

"You should stop the counting and go back to touching."

"Oh. Babe. I'm getting back to it."

And he really just was. His hands were sure, specific, practiced on my body. We'd been together long enough to know what each other liked, and what each other loved. The night before was full of love and passion. Tonight? Would be full of frantic, frenzied, crazy stupid, straight-up fucking.

His hands went from sure and specific to wild and wanton in an instant, pulling me out of the chair suddenly and spinning me suddenly, tugging at my shirt hard enough that the buttons popped. He pressed me into the wall, my face turned slightly, cheek into the herringbone wallpaper I'd agonized over, but never examined this close up. "Oh," was all I managed to get out as his mouth closed around the tendon on the right side of my neck, nipping and tugging as he snapped my pants open and guided them roughly down my thighs.

"Off. Take them off. Take everything off," he said, his voice guttural in my ear, his hands placed on my body, one at my throat and one on my hip. This is why I'd never get tired of Simon. He could go from loving to crazed in an instant, always able to surprise me, keep things interesting. "Off," he reminded me, pulling me out of my head and back into the present. Where I could feel him, hard and insistent, pressing against my backside.

I slipped my jeans down, pushing my panties along with them. I must have been going too slowly, because he suddenly yanked them the rest of the way down, pushing me harder against the wall. I loved sweet and slow Wallbanger, but I loved Wallbanger Wallbanger the best!

With one hand in the center of my back and the other twisted into my hair, he pressed me against the wall, down and out, angling my hips back toward him. I heard his belt unbuckle, then the unzipping, and then I could feel him ready. Always ready. The hand on my back now slipped down to my hips, anchoring me as he shoved my legs farther apart. I gasped as I felt him, exactly where I needed him to be.

"Tell me you want this, you want me," he breathed, heavy in my ear.

"Jesus Christ, Simon, of course I do," I panted as his hand left my hip and traveled to my breast, twisting and turning, pinching sharply and making me gasp once more.

"Tell me you want this," he said again, accenting his words with a final tug, making me arch into him even more, my hips searching for his.

"Yes, Simon! I want this, I want you," I cried out, frantic now for the feel of him inside me. "I always want you."

With one hand still tangled in my hair, keeping me against the wall, his other hand now dipped below, finding me slick and hot and ready for him by his words alone. He groaned at the feel of me on his fingers, and then let out the sexiest groan as he sank inside, inch by perfect inch. I reached back with my hands, trying to bring him closer, to get him further inside, but he placed my hands back on the wall, pulling my hips out farther.

"Look at you—Jesus, just look at you," he moaned, pulling out almost all the way and then slamming inside almost instantly, bowing my back and making me gasp. "So hot like this, you're so sexy . . ."

"When you're fucking me?" I asked, blinking innocently over my shoulder. Which he then bit down on . . . hard. Then he pulled out. Which I barely had time to process, because the next thing I knew he was on the floor between my legs, with his back to the wall, pulling me against his mouth. Hard.

Here's the thing about my fiancé. He loves to take a taste.

His mouth was furious as his tongue licked and lapped at me. One hand was firm against my backside, holding me against his beautiful face as I rocked my hips into him. The other hand held me open to him, keeping me open as the room began to blur and the colors began to run . . .

"Don't stop, don't you dare stop," I chanted as he circled his tongue against me, his lips and his mouth covering me, sucking and biting and licking and kissing and loving and . . .

I exploded. He stayed until I exploded again. And then once more for good measure. And when I was boneless and unable to stand, he pulled me down onto the floor, lifted my legs onto his shoulders, and absolutely wrecked me for any other man.

It's very possible that I passed out on the kitchen floor. Because when I woke moments or hours later,

I was covered by a pea green and orange afghan, and Simon was standing at the kitchen island eating a bowl of Honey Nut Cheerios. Naked.

The week after Simon and I got engaged went by in a blur. I worked, he worked, we told everyone we knew our exciting news and our phones filled with congratulatory emoticons and best wishes. Jillian even had the outgoing message on the overnight answering service at the office changed to announce my engagement. At the end of the message of course, after our address and operating hours were given.

I'd always spoken to my mother often, usually two to three times a week typically. Now she called me every day, multiple times. As early as 7 a.m. and once as late as eleven thirty, when I just had to turn on Jimmy Fallon to see an outfit that Drew Barrymore was wearing and wouldn't it make for a pretty bridesmaid dress? Mimi was unrelenting as well. In her typical bulldog sensibilities, she'd brought every single bridal magazine that was currently in print to my office Monday afternoon, along with her back issues of *Martha Stewart Weddings*, starting around 2002. Took her two hand trucks and three rides in the elevator to bring them all up, but by god she did it.

I was beginning work on a redesign for an existing client of mine over in Dolores Heights, and the time I was supposed to be working on her kitchen remodel

I found myself running interference on a Skype call between my mother and Mimi debating the hotly contested topic of full or partial veils and why a forehead such as mine was able to pull off a more ornate lace fall. I didn't have a clue what any of these things meant, but it was exciting and fun and overwhelming and wonderful all that the same time.

By Friday night I was exhausted, and over takeout Thai food eaten on our living room couch, I told Simon that I absolutely refused to let the planning of our wedding overtake the actual moment that we were celebrating. Our marriage. With a curry-scented kiss on my forehead, Simon shook his head at my naïveté and simply smiled.

Famous last curry.

chapter five

Months later . . .

"Mom, you can't put the Royers by the Boccis, they hate each other. Ever since Mr. Bocci ran over Mrs. Royer's cat. How can you not remember this? Golden Graham got smushed under the front wheel of the Royers' new Mercedes. It was all Mrs. Bocci talked about all summer long, it's why we stopped inviting them to pool parties, because all she wanted to do was talk about her dead cat . . . Yes . . . Yes, summer before I went to college . . . Yes, it's gone on that long . . . Yep, you got it. Put them by the Schaefers, everyone likes them . . . Okay . . . talk to you tomorrow . . . Bye . . . Bye . . . Bye . . ."

I hung up the phone, rubbing my ear. It was hot. It should be. I'd been fielding calls from my mother for the last thirty minutes, after spending the last thirty hours with her in our home.

Our home, which had turned into Wedding Central. My mother had come in for a weekend blitz of wedding details, the likes of which I'd not been the least bit prepared for. My mother, Simon, Mimi, and I, along with Jillian and Sophia for certain portions, had been shuttling across the bay and back again for two days of cake sampling, menu tastings, flower designing, dress fittings, and big band listening. The listening had been my favorite part, actually. The rest? For. The. Birds.

How do people get married without losing their minds? Without losing their wallets? Without being convicted for assault by petticoat? I'd now been front and center for two weddings that I'd been directly involved with, first Jillian and then Mimi. And I'd thought from the outside, even as involved as I'd been, I'd be prepared for the onslaught of decisions and complications and the sheer terror of putting a foot wrong on *our important day.*

I'd been blissfully ignorant. Not this time. I was full metal jacket in the middle of this tulle and lace torture extravaganza and it was going to drive me to the nuthouse. When my mother finally left to drive back home, leaving me in a house stacked with early wedding gifts, seating charts, and maps of the immediate areas surrounding both the church and the reception to help Mimi predict the traffic patterns on *our important day,* I'd closed the front door with a cheery wave and collapsed right there in the entryway. Simon found me there several minutes later when he handed me a cell phone.

"Your mother," he mouthed.

"I turned my phone off!" I mouthed back.

"That explains why she's calling my phone, then, doesn't it?"

"Shit!" I whispered, then took the phone from him. "Hi, Mom, what's up?" I said as he picked up my left ankle and dragged me into the living room. Luckily we'd just had the floor waxed and polished.

Once I hung up the phone, I looked up at him from where he'd left me, just next to the couch where he sat, looking exhausted and more than a little confused.

"She didn't even make it onto the freeway before she thought of more seating chart issues," I explained, handing him back his phone.

"I got that. How can it be so hard to put all these people in the same room? Hi. You're our loved ones. We'd like you to be here with us while we make things official and all that. You're our favorite people in the entire world. We're going to feed you roasted beef tenderloin with new baby potatoes dotted with a mushroom sauce made from mushrooms foraged in the hills above San Francisco. And you can't forget about a dead cat long enough to enjoy the Atlantic prawns served over a bed of sautéed arugula accented with a garlic foam?"

"We had to eighty-six the prawns, babe. Too many people have a shellfish allergy."

"But I loved the garlic foam!"

"I know, babe."

"This is getting out of hand." He sighed, covering

his face. I crawled from the floor up onto his lap and pried his hands back.

"I hear that. Want to elope?"

"Tomorrow," he said, looking at me to see if I was serious. When I shook my head, he sighed again. "It's fine. It'll be good. Then I get you all to myself on a beach in Spain for three weeks."

"You're right about that. I'm so glad you were able to get that same house in Nerja. It's the perfect place for a honeymoon. And it's only a month away."

"A month. Only a month. Only a month," he repeated like a mantra. "I thought I'd get some time to pack this weekend for my trip, but taste testing cakes took precedence."

"They were really good cakes; don't tell me you didn't enjoy that part of it."

"They were good, but nothing's as good as what you make for me. If I had my way, we'd be having your apple pie instead of wedding cake," he said, his hands resting on my hips.

"That's sweet, babe. But the triple coconut with raspberry cream was pretty damn good."

"Agreed. Want to come help me pack?"

I said yes, and then hung off the back of the couch until he picked me up and carried me upstairs piggyback. He had his last trip before the wedding, a two-week shoot in Vietnam. I hated that I couldn't come along. *National Geographic* was sending him to do a study on the newly developed cave system in Son Doong, just opened for tours in the last two years or so, and the hottest ticket in Vietnamese tourism right now. There were entire sections that hadn't been photographed yet, underground rain forests and rivers that hadn't been seen by hardly anyone. Rappelling down rocky slippery cliffs, wading through dark rushing water, dodging bats and bugs the size of dinner plates—it was exactly the kind of thing Simon loved. And he'd capture it on film in his unique way, taking viewers along with him to the deepest, darkest recesses under the earth.

"I still can't believe you can't put this trip off until after the wedding." I sighed, still perched on his back as he navigated the upstairs hallway.

"I think it's more that you can't believe you aren't coming with me," he replied.

"True, but mostly I just wish you were here to help me finish up this last little bit of planning."

"Babe, you've got Frick and Frack the planning twins competing to alphabetize your favors. I think you'll be okay," he said, grabbing his duffel bag from his closet and dropping it onto the bed. He dropped me onto the bed a moment later.

It was true, my mother and Mimi were running things pretty well at this point. And as busy as I'd stayed at work, I was glad for the help. But still, there were last-minute things still to do and he was getting to skip out on some of them.

"Remember when we said this wedding would be about us, and what we wanted?" I asked, watching as T-shirts and shorts went into the bag.

"I think we waved bye-bye to that a few months ago, babe, when we had three separate discussions about Jordan almonds and what color netting they needed to be wrapped in."

"I know, I know. I don't even like almonds. But it's . . . I mean . . . it's still us, right?"

"Yes, it's still us. Us, and three hundred of our closest friends."

"Ugh. Three hundred. It sounds insane when I say it, but when I go through the list, I don't know who we'd cut out at this point," I cried, laying back against the pillows. The guest list had ballooned up and up until it was beyond ridiculous. Most of Simon's old school pals and their wives were coming west for the wedding, which was wonderful to see. His childhood neighbors, the Whites, were coming as well. He was very happy when he saw their RSVP.

"How many Jillian Design clients are on the list? How many of your parents' friends made the cut? There's tons of people on there that we don't know. Don't know well, let's say."

"Let's not have this discussion again, okay?" The guest list, the menu, the parking attendants, everything was just getting bigger and bigger. And the bigger it became, the more I could tell Simon was putting on his game face, making it seem like he was okay with everything. But when it was just the two of us, and the planning committee had retired for the night, he admitted it was a bit overwhelming. But he was in for a penny, in for a pound, and insisted we keep everything as it was. But that didn't mean he didn't get a little disgruntled from time to time. We'd had several tense conversations over the last few months, mostly over the guest list. He didn't understand, not coming from a large family that all lived within an hour of where we now lived, why it was necessary to invite so many people.

Mostly, though, I think seeing how many guests were in his column, and how many were in my column was difficult to see. It was like a black-and-white reminder of who he'd lost. And who wouldn't be there. He was a trooper. He was my trooper.

And it was all happening in a month. And then we could begin to live our lives again, just for us. And our little kitty family. I changed the subject, asking him questions about his trip and getting the details on what he'd be doing. And as we talked, the tension eased. As his bag filled up and the cats began to circle, knowing that this was what happened before Daddy went on a trip, we talked only of cameras and caves, and no more tulle and lace.

And when we went to bed that night, and he kissed me long and deep and told me he loved me and he'd miss my sweet ass while I was gone, I giggled and let him love on me as long as he could. Which was awhile, because this was my Wallbanger we were talking about here.

Early the next morning, I drove him to the airport, kissed him good-bye, told him I wasn't wearing any panties, and then kissed him once more while he tried to push me back into the car to see if I was bluffing. I was not. Kissing him a final time, I told him I loved him and I'd see him in two weeks.

No one ever tells you to remember these moments. To photograph them in your mind, develop them into memories, to have them easily accessible and on instant recall when you'd need them later. To try and replay and re-create the last time you see someone.

It was 2 a.m. I was asleep on the couch under a cover of furry bodies. Food Network was on the television. I unstuck my face from the pillow . . . nice. Drool. Wait, why was I on the couch? And what was ringing? The phone. Oh, the phone! I scrambled to pick it up, seeing it was Simon.

"Babe? You make it there?"

"Just landed in Hanoi," he said, yawning, but his voice had the sense of urgency he always has when he's on a trip. He loved his work. He loved the travel. There was a time when we first started living together that he wasn't traveling as much, and I thought he might be thinking about giving up this globe-trotting life. He still traveled, just not as much. But he loved it too much to ever give it up. And I loved him too much to ever ask him to. Besides, we were used to being apart. It's how we met, it's how we got together, it's how we fell in love. We made it work, because it was all we knew.

"How was the flight?"

"Last leg was brutal, but it's good to be here. Sun's shining, it's a thousand degrees, and there's a bowl of pho waiting for me as soon as I get off this phone."

"Well, don't let me keep you," I teased. "Thanks for checking in. When are you heading to the first location?"

"Tomorrow morning. I'm spending the day in the city, acclimating and working with the guys here who are taking me out with the tour. Then hopping on the night train tomorrow. Or tonight. I have no idea what time it is."

"Okay, babe, call me when you can." I knew he'd check in, but when Simon was working he tended to lose all track of time. He certainly was the same way when he was working me . . .

"Will do. Love you."

"Love you too. Ella says she misses you."

"Aw, tell my pretty girl I miss her too."

"She only sleeps with me when you're out of town."

"She knows who's in charge."

"Hanging up on you, Wallbanger."

"Hanging up on you first, Nightie—"

Hee-hee. I got there first. Dislodging four cats took some doing, but eventually I was on my feet and stretching before heading up to bed. My phone beeped, and I looked down at the screen. He'd sent me a picture of his noodles. Ass.

I worked hard that week, trying to stack up some work ahead of time before the big day. Monica had transitioned from assistant to junior designer since coming on board last year, and she'd been instrumental in helping me, and the entire team, move seamlessly into the new arrangement we had with Jillian's new schedule. Monica still worked closely with me on most of my accounts, but she was beginning to take on some small projects on her own, usually with me looking on in an advisory role. She'd been handling my clients while I was on wedding lockdown. Knowing she'd be keeping things up in the air and moving while I was gone was a huge help, but I still wanted to make sure I could get as much done as I could before *our important day*.

By the end of the week I was exhausted, but feeling like I'd gotten a little bit ahead. I had a meeting at four thirty with Jillian that I had a feeling would end in drinks afterward. I had that feeling because it was how we ended almost every single week when she was in town, so I felt pretty sure about that feeling. The fact that I was carrying a bottle of wine was also a tip-off. I was headed down to her office, arms full of binders and my always-present colored pencils, along with the wine, when I heard her raising her voice to someone on the phone.

"Oh my God, are you sure? What does that mean? Jesus, what am I supposed to tell her?"

I poked my head around the corner, not wanting to interrupt her but not wanting her to think I was eavesdropping either. "Should I come back?" I whispered. She looked at me, and when my eyes met hers the hairs on the back of my neck stood up. Her eyes were wide, and panicked, and filling with tears. The room narrowed, my field of vision now only including her face and that phone. "What's going on?" I asked, my voice trembling. Because I knew, you see.

"Caroline, sweetie, it's Benjamin," she started, and my blood turned to an icy burn. It was only later that I realized I'd dropped everything I was carrying. Including the wine, which dropped squarely on my big toe. I had a bruise under the nail for months.

"What's going on?" I heard someone say, and the someone was me.

"I don't know, he just called and—"

"Give me the phone, Jillian," I said, crossing to her in an instant and grabbing the phone out of her hand. "Where is he? What's wrong?"

"I don't know anything yet, Caroline. I—"

"If you didn't know anything you wouldn't be calling Jillian, and she wouldn't be gray right now. What's happened to Simon?" I asked, my voice now rising higher and higher. I sounded shrill, I sounded desperate. I sounded scared to death.

"I don't know much, one of the guys he was with called me. I'm listed as his emergency contact still with *National Geographic* I guess. There was an accident in one of the caves today. It's so hard to understand what happened; the guy doesn't exactly speak fluent English and the reception was so spotty and—"

"Goddammit, Benjamin, what happened?" I yelled, slamming my hand down on Jillian's desk.

"He fell. He was on some kind of bamboo scaffolding, and the wire he was attached to wasn't secure, and he fell. I don't know how far. Enough to maybe break some bones."

"Broken bones. Okay, maybe broken bones." I exhaled, clutching the desk now as my knees wobbled. "Okay, okay," I repeated.

"Not just that, Caroline, he was knocked out by the fall. There's been some kind of damage to his skull. They airlifted him to a hospital, but as far as I can tell he's still unconscious. I don't know much more than that. I've been trying to reach one of the doctors treating him but—"

"Monica!" I yelled down the hall. "Get in here right now!"

"Caroline, what are you doing?" Jillian asked, and I held up a finger.

"Benjamin, I need to know where he is. What city,

what hospital. I need a doctor's name. I need his fixer's name and his contact information," I said to Benjamin, just as Monica was running into the office.

"Caroline, good lord woman, a simple Monica come on in here would have been—"

"Do you still have my passport information from when you helped me book our trip to Spain?" I asked, telling Benjamin to hold on.

"Yeah, yeah I should," she said, looking from me to Jillian. "What's going on?"

"I need you to book me on the first flight to Hanoi. Just give me an hour to get home and grab my passport. Text me the information when you have it."

"Wait, Hanoi? When? How much am I allowed to spend? Where do you want to connect through? How—"

"As soon as possible. I don't care. I don't care. Please do this now," I replied, now calm. "Benjamin, I'm leaving the office to go home and get my passport and then I'm heading for the airport. Jillian's going to drive me so I can make some calls on the way. Find out what you can and call me as soon as you know more, okay?"

"Okay, you got it. You sure you want to—"

"You're telling me that Simon is unconscious somewhere in the world. What the hell would I be doing right now?" I asked, handing the phone back to Jillian and heading for the door. "I'll be ready to leave in two minutes. Monica, get me on a plane."

• • •

Five hours later, I was on a plane over the Pacific. One seat left. First class. Do you have any idea how much a last-minute first-class ticket to Asia costs? Just start typing zeros, just line those fuckers up.

I sat in my pod, not watching a movie. Did you know in first class on those Asian flights you get your own damn pod? It's like a minisuite, but on a plane. When Simon and I went to Vietnam awhile back, we flew business class. Sure, it was super nice, but it wasn't like this.

Monica had to split it over five credit cards. I didn't care. I was on my way to Simon. Benjamin had been able to get me some additional information before my flight took off. Still unconscious, he was being tested for what they called TBI, or traumatic brain injury. If there was swelling around the brain from a skull fracture, which Benjamin said they had not yet ruled out, he would likely need surgery to relieve the intercranial pressure.

Let me tell you what you should never do. Never go to WebMD and do a search for any of these terms. You will scare yourself silly. As it was, I was trying very hard to stay off the in-flight wi-fi doing exactly this. I kept checking my phone only for updates or emails from Benjamin, who still had nothing new to report.

So I sat in my pod and I thought. About my sweet Simon. Benjamin had called the hospital and spoken with the staff, letting them know that while I was technically not listed as next of kin or even as an emergency contact (something that would be rectified as soon as possible), that I was his fiancée and should be allowed to see him when I arrived at the hospital. Benjamin had also been given power of attorney when it came to Simon, something that had been established years before, when he was still at Stanford. My sweet Simon, totally alone in the world for years except for Benjamin, as he globe-trotted this way and that, not a care in the world other than his beloved photography. With Benjamin back in San Francisco, managing his finances and his sole contact in case there ever was an emergency, he was truly untethered.

But not anymore. I was his tether. I was his contact. I was his in-case-of-emergency everything, or I should be. I loved him more than any person currently on this planet, and I was terrified that something was going to happen to him before I could get there.

I sat in my pod, high above the ocean, and as my brain kept burning and churning, the thought I kept bumping into was garlic foam. The garlic foam on giant prawns that he wanted served at our wedding, but he couldn't have them. Somewhere along the line, it was decided that our guests who might be allergic to shellfish were more important than what the groom wanted to eat at his own wedding.

What the fuck? How had this happened? Things become very clear when you're sitting in a pod over the ocean thinking about your sweet Simon. And the fact was, I didn't give a flying fuck about any of that wedding nonsense. I just wanted to say the same words to this man that people had been saying for generations and generations. I wanted to stand up with this man and make sure he knew that he was mine and I was his for better or for worse, in sickness and in health, as long as we both shall live. And the rest? Bull to the shit.

You can't pace on an airplane for very long before you start making people nervous, so I sat in my pod and I didn't watch the movie but I did watch the movie that was playing on the inside of my eyelids. Simon, the first time I saw him. Half naked, covered only in a sheet, standing on the other side of his front door, annoyed that I'd been banging on his door, but not so annoyed that he didn't check out my legs peeking out from beneath that pink nightie. Simon, the first time I kissed him. Standing on Jillian's terrace under the moonlight with the waves crashing and the crickets cricketing and my hands full of his stupid awesome-smelling sweater and my lips full of his. Simon, the first time he made love to me. In the most beautiful bed in the most beautiful bedroom in the most beautiful house in Spain, where he held himself above me, shaking with need as he moved inside of me. Simon, the first time he fucked me. Surrounded by raisins and covered in flour as I rode him hard, and we welcomed back my long-lost but not forgotten orgasm.

Simon, the day he asked me to buy our house with him. Sitting with me on his lap in the corner of our now bedroom, walls covered in hideous wallpaper as he poured his heart out all over the terrible carpet, asking me to make a home with him. Simon, dancing with me to a big band at the opening of my first hotel I'd designed. Simon, devouring my zucchini bread. Simon, searching for hours in the rain for Clive. Simon, sleeping in the corner of our bed snoring louder than anything legal.

Simon, standing in the shower asking me to be his wife. Simon was my world. And I was traveling around this one to get to him. In time.

chapter six

I landed in Hanoi with a phone full of messages from Mimi, Sophia, Ryan, and Neil, but I listened only to the ones that came in from Benjamin. Simon had woken up, albeit briefly. He was still heavily sedated, and was getting ready to go in for another MRI to determine whether he'd need surgery. Depending on how quickly I could get to the hospital, I might be there for the results. I managed to get through customs without screaming, stuffed my overnight bag into a broken-down taxi, and barked out orders to take me to Hanoi French Hospital, where Simon was being treated.

This entire time, I hadn't cried a tear. Not when I called my parents to tell them where I was going. Not when I packed a bag in such hurry that I ended up with ten pairs of pants, and only two pairs of actual panties. Not when Jillian dropped me off at the airport, and not when I barricaded myself in the first-class lounge ladies' room, the first place I could be alone and where I'd already given myself permission to fall apart. But no tears.

And now as I rode pell-mell across the crowded streets of Hanoi, heading toward this hospital, still no tears. But the panic was beginning to build. I'd been running on sheer adrenaline until this point, but since my phone died and I hadn't been able to get any new information, I was ready to come out of my skin.

We pulled into the hospital and I gave the driver at least five times as much as he needed because I hadn't yet converted anything over from U.S. currency, but I didn't care. I raced inside, looking for a directory of any kind. Neurology. Benjamin had said he'd be in neurology. But he also said intensive care . . . so where did I go? Where was he? I spun in place, looking for anyone who might be able to help me.

"Miss?" a soft voice asked, and I turned to see someone sitting at an information desk. "May I help you?"

She had a southern accent, for pity's sake. I don't know what I was expecting, racing into a Vietnamese hospital, but a tiny blonde who sounded like Delta Burke wasn't it.

"I'm looking for a patient, Simon Parker. I'm his fiancée, and he was in an accident. I was told he was here? But I don't know where, or which floor, or—"

"Simon Parker, yes, he's here. He's up on the fourth floor. Would you like me to take you up there?"

I burst into tears, giant, shaking, sobbing tears. I couldn't help it, my body simply let go all at once and everything poured out of my eyeballs. "Yes. Please," I managed as she handed me several tissues, and then finally the entire box.

"Simon Parker, he's the photographer, right?"

"Yes!" I warbled, letting her lead me toward the elevator. "How did you know?"

"We only have so many American patients here at a time. The staff sort of knows who's who pretty quick. Took a fall, right?"

"Yes! But I haven't spoken to anyone since I landed. How is he? Do you know?" I asked, wiping my face as the elevator door opened on the fourth floor.

"I think you better talk to his doctor. Let me get you to his room, okay?" she said, ushering me toward the nurses' station. Once there, she spoke quickly to the nurses, who pointed us toward a room. Not even bothering to thank her, I raced for the door, seeing his name on the chart just outside.

I prepared myself. I took a deep breath, steeled myself for whatever I might find inside, and opened the door. Strong, strong, strong. I'd be strong. Whatever I found on the other side of that door, I'd be strong for him.

Yeah. Not so much. Because when I saw Simon lying in a hospital bed, surrounded by tubes and machines and buttons and beeping, I almost came out of my skin. He lay there with bandages wrapped around his head— asleep? Unconscious? It didn't matter, I was grateful for two things. One, that he wasn't awake to see me fall apart against the doorjamb. When he did wake up—and there was no "if," only when—he'd find a pulled-together Caroline. And two, and more important, I was just . . . grateful. Grateful that I was here, now, with Simon. So I allowed myself two more minutes of losing it, said the quickest of thanks to whoever might be listening, then swept his hair back from his forehead, gently, barely touching his skin. His face was covered in tiny cuts and scrapes, butterfly bandages covering the deeper ones on his left cheekbone. Bruises bloomed here and there, and down along his neck and upper torso, surgical tape was wrapped tightly. I let my breath out in a slow shudder, then pressed the tiniest of kisses on a cheek that still smelled familiar even under all the antiseptic. Then I started looking for a nurse, a doctor, anyone with a stethoscope who could tell me what was going on.

I checked in at the nurses' station. Benjamin had already made sure that I was cleared as a visitor, and that I could speak with the doctor as fully as he could. Since Benjamin retained power of attorney, he'd have to be the one to communicate with the hospital staff if any decisions needed to be made. I knew that any decision would be made with me, but my brain could only accommodate this thought in the abstract, not as something that would actually happen.

I spoke with the doctor who was caring for Simon, and he explained more about what Benjamin had told me. They were waiting for the results from his most recent MRI. Simon had been waking up intermittently all morning, and if I wanted to catch him when he was awake, I could stay in his room, and the doctor would come get me when the results came in.

So I did just that. I checked in with Benjamin back home, plopped my bag down, sat in the chair next to Simon's bed, and watched him sleep. I held his hand, marveling once more at the length of his fingers, the strength in his hand, the handsomeness of just his fore-arm. I ran my fingertips up and down his arm absently as I held his hand, watching as his eyelids fluttered a bit. Was he dreaming? What did he dream about? Likely the photo he was getting when he took his fall . . .

As I was thinking these random thoughts, I felt his hand squeeze mine, as it had done a thousand times before. I looked from our hands to his face, where those sapphire eyes were open and blinking at me.

"Hey," I whispered, and watched as his eyes wan-dered confusedly for a moment, then focused on mine.

"Hey, babe," he whispered back, and my eyes filled with tears. *Hey* and *babe* were now officially the most beautiful words in the English language. "You look pretty." Go ahead and add three more words to that list.

"I'll grab your nurse, okay?" I said, reaching for the call button.

"So glad you're here," he murmured, and was back to sleep before the nurse even left her chair at the station. But that was okay.

Simon slipped between asleep and awake the rest of that day, and most of the night. The last round of scans showed that although he had suffered a significant concussion, the effects would not be lasting and he'd have a full recovery. Benjamin spoke with the doctor as well, confirming that I'd be staying with Simon at the hospital until he was ready to be released.

Simon finally began to really wake up around three in the morning, preceded by the funniest twenty minutes of my life. Wallbanger on pain meds isn't like any show I've ever seen. Starting with:

"Hey. Caroline. Did I ever tell you how much I love you?"

"All the time, babe, but I never get tired of hearing it."

"I'll say it more often."

"Sure, Simon. You can tell me whenever you like."

"Hey. Caroline. Did I ever tell you how much I love you?"

"You sure did, about two minutes ago."

"What's a minute?"

This also happened . . .

"And at the bottom of the cave, it was like, the world opened up, and there were stars . . . but it was like . . . we were the stars . . . there were stars everywhere, but like . . . we were the stars . . . and you know what else?"

"What's that, Simon?'

"We were them."

"What?"

"Them."

"Them?"

"The stars. . . . we were them . . . the stars . . ."

And if you liked that, you'll love . . .

"Babies. I want to fill you up with babies. Like, make you pregnant with babies. And have some of the babies. Babies. Babies. Caroline? Babies."

And finally . . .

"Caroline, I'm so glad you're here. But why'd you bring so many leprechauns?"

My stomach hurt from trying hard not to laugh at how silly he was on pain meds. But as they wore off into something a little more manageable, he began to make a little more sense. He sipped at some water that I held, nodding when he was through.

"Go ahead and lay back; you shouldn't sit up so straight," I said, urging him back against his pillow. The doctor said he might be dizzy for a while.

"I'm good right now, actually." He frowned, watching as I stretched my back out. "How're you feeling? Don't you want to get some sleep?"

"I slept on the plane."

"You did not, you never sleep on planes," he corrected.

Caught, I smiled ruefully.

"I'm fine—really. Tell me how you're feeling. Are you super sore?"

"A little, yeah," he admitted.

"And the rib?" I asked.

"Rib?"

"You cracked a rib, and a bunch more are bruised," I said.

"I did?"

My eyes widened. "How much do you remember?"

"All of it. At least, I think I do," he said, his eyes searching as he remembered. "Oh yeah, I bet I did crack a rib."

"You tell me everything that happened. Right now," I said, reaching for his hand and holding it tightly. "And don't you dare leave anything out."

He told me about the incredible cave and the scale of photographing such an amazing natural space. And of the rickety bamboo structure he used to scramble over to get his motherfucking photos. And the fact that he was hurrying to get the last bit of light before they had to move on to another shot. And the fact that he was not entirely secured into the safety harness he'd agreed to wear. And the fact that he tumbled ass over camera more than fifty feet down the side of a limestone cliff, knocking himself out in the process, and bringing down most of the scaffolding with him. He remembered falling, he remembered hitting the floor of the cave, and he remembered he'd saved the camera from any serious damage. Unbelievable. He also remembered how sure he was that he'd gotten the shot. Double unbelievable.

My tears had started again somewhere during the story, and now I sat next to him on the bed, holding his hand tightly and refusing to look anywhere but directly at him. Taking in his face, his hands, his arms, his legs, his toes twitching underneath the hospital blanket. I touched him wherever I could, wherever he didn't have a bruise or a cut, which didn't give me a lot of space to work with. But I held him as best as I could, and I stroked his hair lightly and I kissed between the scrapes and I told him how much I loved him. I couldn't help it. And in between it all, with me comforting him, he of course held on to me as tightly as he could. Whispering words like, "I'm okay, babe," and, "Everything's going to be fine," and, "Don't cry."

The *don't cry* tipped me over the edge. Because now, with him in my arms as much as he could be, I was finally feeling everything I'd fought to keep at bay. My panic, my terror, my helplessness, my horror at going through life without him next to me, cracking jokes and copping a feel.

"I could kill you, you know," I said suddenly, breaking free of his hold and sitting back to look at him in the eye. "Seriously. I love you, and I love what you do, and I would never ask you to give it up. But you're not a cartoon superhero, with a devil-may-care smile on your face as you wrestle fucking lions before lunch, just to get the shot. Okay? If you ever do something like this again, get hurt because you're getting the fucking shot, I will kill you myself," I said, pointing my finger. "Without pain meds."

"I promise, I'll be more careful," he said, telling me what I wanted to hear, but also promising me with his eyes that he was taking what I said seriously.

"I love you so much," I said, threading my fingers through his, still needing the contact.

"I love you too," he said, his voice becoming thick as the fresh round of pain meds kicked in. "So glad you're here."

"Eh, I wanted to come back here anyway. Maybe we could go spelunking?"

He chuckled, which made his ribs hurt, but he continued to smile. Which made me finally smile.

By the end of that very long day, which started for me on the other side of the world, Simon was feeling much better. By the end of that week, Simon was released from the hospital. The guy was born under some kind of lucky star. He had to continue to take it easy, with lots of rest and light activity, but he was cleared for release. The doctors recommended that we stay for at least another few days before attempting to fly home. Flying after sustaining a concussion, especially one as severe as the one Simon had, could prove uncomfortable at best. Seizures and nausea at worst, so I made the decision to stay over as long as we needed to, making sure he was up to such a long flight.

After spending that first night in the city, I hired a driver and took him away to recuperate. There was an island we'd explored one afternoon the last time we'd been to Ha Long Bay, and I'd been fascinated by the accommodations there. A tiny hotel, remote and isolated. More of a collection of luxury bungalows than a hotel, it offered the kind of piece and quiet we needed. Each bungalow was situated on the beach, with gorgeous sea views all around. There were sumptuous beds, complete with requisite mosquito netting, European-style bathrooms, and twenty-four-hour room service. The drive was only a few hours, followed by a short boat cruise to the hotel.

When we docked, I helped to make sure the luggage was carried straight to our bungalow, and we headed inside to get checked in.

"This is incredible, babe, but unnecessary. We could have stayed in the city, wouldn't have been a problem."

"I realize that, Simon, but since we were here, your very dramatic accident and all, I thought we'd treat ourselves a little bit. Have a few days of rest and relaxation before heading back home."

"A prehoneymoon honeymoon?" he said, bumping my hips with his own, his hands resting lightly on my waist.

"Something like that." I smiled, but shook my head. "But no honey with this moon; you heard the doctor," I said, and Simon growled. He had delicately suggested that certain things should wait perhaps until Simon had fully recovered from his accident. Between the cracked rib and the head dent, I was in full agreement. Simon was not.

"You wait and see. Tonight, when the breeze starts

blowing and the waves start lapping at the sand, you'll change your mind," he murmured, sweeping my hair up to kiss the back of my neck. "Besides, you know I look good in the moonlight. You'll be all about getting into my pants."

"Uh, yes, here are your keys, Miss Reynolds." I felt Simon tense behind me as I smiled at the desk clerk.

"Yes, thank you so much." I smiled, smothering a laugh.

"You'll be in bungalow seven; just follow the path. Your luggage should already be there."

"Thank you," Simon piped up from behind me, and this time I didn't smother anything. Gathering up my purse and the keys, I took him by the hand and led him back out onto the beach. It was late in the afternoon, almost evening, and the light was beginning to change, taking on that magical glow that twilight seems to have. All the edges soften, the colors bleed, and even the air changes a bit. A warm breeze was blowing in off the sea, bringing with it a salty tang that crinkled my tongue. We passed six other bungalows along the rock-lined path, finally coming around a bend to see our own. Lit with hurricane candles, with white linen curtains puffing through the windows, it looked like heaven. Heaven . . . with the option of air-conditioning. Which in the tropics was sometimes a very good thing.

"Hey look, no neighbors," Simon said, scanning the corner of the beach we'd been given. It was true, there wasn't another soul to be seen. A light or two peeked through the trees here and there, hinting at other humans, but other than that it was us and the waves.

"Let's check it out," I said, tugging him by the hand and up onto the porch. Deep, comfy-looking chairs anchored by pillows flanked the ornately carved front door. "Here's the key, open it, would you? I'm going to see if these chairs are as comfortable as they look."

"Sure thing," he said, taking the key from me and turning it in the lock. Just before he pushed open the door, it opened from the inside. "What the—"

Benjamin stood in the doorway. Jillian stood next to him. Both were smiling.

"Wait a minute, how did you guys get— What's going on?" he asked, looking back and forth between them and me. I just grinned.

"Good to see you're still in one piece," Benjamin said, pulling a still-surprised Simon into a fierce hug. "And don't ever do that to me again, you hear me?"

"Move over, move over," Jillian said, sweeping her husband aside to grab on to Simon and wrap her arms around him as well. "So, so, so glad you're okay. No more caves, promise me that!"

"Hey, watch the ribs," Simon protested, confused but still happy to see them. "But seriously, what are you guys doing here?"

"We came over to make sure Caroline had everything she needed. She kind of took off like a bat out of hell when she found out you'd decided to examine the cave with your face. That's a bossy girl you got there," Benjamin said, wrapping an arm around his shoulders and walking him back down the steps to the sand. "Come on back with me to our bungalow; we're just down the beach, I'll tell you all about it. Let the ladies settle in a bit."

"Okay, yeah, sure. Caroline, you good with that?" Simon asked, still curious.

"Go ahead, Jillian brought me some things, new changes of clothes and stuff. I'll powwow with her and then we can all head back up to the main house for dinner, sound good?" I nodded, walking over to the front of the porch, leaning down to kiss him once, then twice.

"Sounds good, babe," he said. "Did you know they were coming?"

"I did," I said, kissing him once more. "Surprise."

"You're kind of terrific, you know that?"

"I do know that," I nodded, then turned him back around. "Go play with Benjamin, I'll see you in a bit."

The pair of them walked off down the beach, and I turned to Jillian.

"Thank you so much for coming all this way."

"You got it. I've always wanted to see this part of the world. And Benjamin has been pacing up a storm. He hated not being over here," she replied, looping her arm through mine and walking with me inside. She handed me an overnight bag I recognized from home.

"Did you bring it?" I asked, unzipping the bag.

"I did," she nodded, and watched as I pulled a long flowing dress from the bag. A long flowing *white* dress.

"Perfect."

An hour later, Simon and Benjamin came out of the bungalow to find Jillian and me waiting for them.

"Hey, where have you— Hey. You look gorgeous," he said, whistling. I stood before him in my white dress, thanked him for the compliment, took his hand, and walked with him down to the beach, leaving our friends behind.

"What's going on? Aren't we going to dinner with those guys?" he asked.

"Not just yet," I answered, looking ahead to the beach, where I could see a few candles lit and a tiki torch or two. "I wanted to talk to you, before they join us."

"What are you up to, Caroline?" he asked, looking carefully at me.

"I bought this dress a year ago in a little boutique in Mendocino, when I was visiting Viv. I was on my way out of town, and I was stopped at a light when I saw it in the window across the street. I couldn't take my eyes off of it. And without having any reason to wear it, and not a clue why I was doing it, I bought it, straight off the mannequin. It didn't even fit me. I had to take it to a tailor to have the hem lengthened; it was too short for me. The tailor told me it was vintage, probably from sometime in the 1930s."

"It looks great on you," he said, holding me at arm's length to get a better look. "Go on, gimme a little twirl."

I laughed, and then twirled. The dress was ivory, bedecked with old lace along the bodice, with a gauzy lace overlay along the skirt. An afternoon dress, it was made for lazy strolls in town, or a trip to the gardens. It was likely worn with stockings and lace-up shoes. I was rocking it barefoot. And in those bare feet, I tugged on his hand once more and continued on the path toward the beach.

"When Benjamin told me something had happened to you, I went into crisis-management mode. I didn't think about anything other than getting to you. To have you that far away, and not be able to know exactly what was wrong or how to help you—I can't think of the words to tell you how that felt. How it felt to have someone you love so much possibly taken away from you." I stopped then, just before the pebbles gave way to sand. "But then, I don't have to give you words. Because you already know what that's like."

A stormy expression stole across his face, and he grasped both of my hands in his. "Caroline, I'm so sorry that you had to go through all of that."

"No no, it's actually fine," I said, stepping into his arms and bringing them around my waist. "Because here's the thing. I had hours in an airplane, with nothing to do and no one to talk to, and the only thing I could think about was you. And us. And how much I love you." I walked him, pushed him really, backward through the sand. "I also thought a lot about something else."

"What's that?" He raised an eyebrow.

"Garlic foam," I answered, then spun him to face the beach.

I love me a speechless Wallbanger.

Hundreds of candles. Tiki torches dancing as far as the eye could see. Lanterns in shades of violet, indigo, emerald, and ruby bumping around on the breeze. The evening breakers splashing lazily against the beach. In the distance, an early moon lit up Ha Long Bay, with its ancient islands and peaks covered in mist and moss. And before us? An aisle lined with votives . . . with Jillian and Benjamin standing at the end of it. Along with them, the Vietnamese equivalent of a justice of the peace.

"Marry me, Simon. Marry me right here, right now, without any bullshit. Marry me, with just our two friends to see it happen. No parents, no work friends, no clients, no peppercorn-encrusted blah-blah, just you and me and the stars. I spent a night in a pod wondering if I was ever going to see your eyes staring back at me again, and I can't manage that again unless I'm your fucking wife. And I don't give one tiny shit about a big fancy wedding, especially without you getting to have your garlic foam. Which, I'd like to point out, is waiting for you back in the main house, for what I hope is our wedding dinner of giant prawns. I want you, only you, for the rest of my life," I said, lips trembling but knees strong. "Marry me, Simon."

He paused, the corner of his mouth lifting as he looked around at the fairy tale laid out in front of him. The fairy tale that was exactly right for *us*. On this very important day.

"One question," he said, lifting our clasped hands to his lips and placing a kiss right below my engagement ring.

"Hit me."

"What was that about spending a night in a pod?"

"Seriously? I ask you to marry me, and that's the line you picked out?"

"Technically, I asked you to marry me first. Let us never forget this very important bit of information."

"So noted."

"Can I ask another question?"

"Just one more, and then I'll need an answer."

"Is this even legal?"

I laughed, then pulled him down to me for a soft kiss. "Not in the slightest. This is just for us."

"You realize you own me, don't you, Nightie Girl?"

"Is that a yes?"

"Hell yes it's a yes, let's get hitched," he whispered, and I threw my arms around his neck. "Watch the rib, okay?"

"Shit!" I exclaimed, and then I heard Benjamin clearing his throat. "Dammit, I just swore at my own wedding. Dammit, I did it again."

"That's three times."

"Can it, Wallbanger."

And with those revered words, we walked ourselves down the aisle. Spoke the simplest of vows. Promised each other everything we could. Kissed under the stars. High-fived our witnesses on the way back down the aisle. Cut the strings on about fifty sky lanterns and set them loose towards the stars. Then headed inside for garlic foam.

Because that's what my husband wanted.

Later that night, in the honeymoon bed . . .

"That feels amazing. Don't stop what you're doing there, please don't stop. Right there. Right there. That's it . . . mmmm."

"How many is that?"

"I've lost count."

"This is the big one."

"I can feel it. Jesus that's good . . . more . . . more . . . more."

"We're going to run out of calamine lotion at this rate."

Here's the thing about getting married outside in the tropics. Mosquitos. Big fuckers. We spent our wedding night scratching each other's bites and applying calamine lotion by the gallon. And with Simon still on the disabled list sexy-times-wise, we spooned, scratched, and watched *Goonies*. With subtitles.

Best. Wedding. Night. Ever.

"Do you, Caroline, take this man, Simon, to be your lawfully wedded husband? To have and to hold, for richer or for poorer, in sickness and in health, for as long as you both shall live?"

"I do."

"And do you, Simon, take this woman, Caroline, to be your lawfully wedded wife? To have and to hold, for richer or for poorer, in sickness and in health, for as long as you both shall live?"

"I do."

And so we made it legal. Simon and I had our very best friends and our very favorite family members over to our house in Sausalito, along with a judge I'd done a remodel for. Simon wore jeans, I wore a sundress, and we got married for a second time. This one recognized by the U.S. government. Were my parents disappointed they didn't get to throw me the huge splashy wedding they'd been planning? Maybe a little, but ultimately they understood. As did Mimi and Sophia, and why they didn't even know about our Vietnamese wedding until after we'd flown home.

We kept our original wedding date, slashed the

guest list by two-thirds, and with the exception of Simon's friends from Pennsylvania and his old neighbors the Whites, everyone was local. At least local to Northern California. Viv and Clark were there, with Will in attendance as well, cute as a button in a tuxedo onesie. And Chloe and Lucas were there too, in town visiting Sophia and Neil. And get this, Chloe and Clark were cousins. How's that for six degrees of Wallbanger? I was happy to have them all here on this very special day. This very special *casual* day. Because in the end, it wasn't the lace and the tulle that made a wedding— it was about the couple saying their I do's, and their friends and family being there to celebrate it with them. We threw a barbecue, opened up a bunch of wine and cold beer, set up a makeshift soda fountain to make egg creams and sundaes, and had a party. We dragged Simon's old record player out onto the terrace, he did some audio nerd stuff with the speakers, and big-band music filled the Sausalito night.

Instead of having a wedding cake, I'd spent two solid days this week in the kitchen with my mom, my girlfriends, my aunts, and my cousins, and we made pans and pans of Ina's Outrageous Brownies. She would have been proud. But for Simon, I made him is very own apple pie, which he smeared all over my face in place of wedding cake. We had wedding pie. Fitting.

I sat on a bench at the edge of our lawn, eating brownies with Mimi and Sophia and watched as our guys played Frisbee with Benjamin and Simon's high school crew. I'd been holding Mary Jane until Sophia had to take over. Someone was hungry.

"Not really the wedding I pictured you having, Caroline," Sophia said, switching boobs. "But it's pretty fun."

"Fun, I'll take. Fancy, I'll leave to you. How's the planning coming along?"

"It's coming along great! The binder is really filling out nicely," Mimi said, interrupting. She was seriously considering starting a second business, and she should. She was damn good at it. "Speaking of the binder, I've got pictures to go through with you on ideas I had for your hair, Sophia. I've been cutting out stuff from magazines for weeks now. Did you know that Grace Sheridan has your exact same hair color and length? Hers is a little more curly than yours, but it's essentially the same."

"Who's Grace Sheridan?" Sophia asked, and Mimi and I both looked at her in surprise.

"You totally know who she is," I said, shaking my head. "She's on that TV show."

"I totally do *not* know who she is. *Sesame Street* and Neil's broadcasts, that's all I ever watch anymore. My brain is mush," Sophia said, shaking her head right back at me.

"Okay, I got this," Mimi said. "She's Jack Hamilton's girlfriend. You know, the—"

"—the Brit? Hello, now I'm right there with you. Holy shit, he is hot. We have to go see the new *Time* movie when it comes out; we'll let the boys stay home with

Mary Jane while we go have some sweet British hunky time," Sophia said, already plotting her girls' night out.

"Yes yes, she's with Jack Hamilton, but more importantly, she's got great hair. And it's exactly the same shade of red as yours. So I found this picture of her on the red carpet and—"

Sophia interrupted Mimi again, unable to stop herself. "—when she walked with Jack down the red carpet? Ahhh! I fucking loved that! Remember how everyone was gossiping about who he was dating?"

"But wait, we were talking about her hair! Listen to me, I've got the perfect updo based on—"

"Oh updo this, let's talk about Jack Hamilton's hair instead. It always looks freshly fucked, you know what I mean? I wonder if they do it in the limo on the way to appearances . . ."

"Stop it—just stop it! We're talking wedding hair here, dammit, and—"

I tuned them out mostly, drinking my beer and listening with one ear as Sophia and Mimi began a heated conversation about updos versus long and flouncy. The other ear was tuned to the Glenn Miller currently crackling through the speakers. And within seconds, Simon appeared.

"Mrs. Parker?" he said, extending his hand.

"Mr. Reynolds." I winked and stood. "Bye, girls."

"Bye," they said in unison as I followed my husband out onto the impromptu dance floor. Taking a cue from our original, if not technically legal, ceremony we had lanterns hung all over the backyard, bringing a little bit of fairy tale home with us from Ha Long Bay.

"Are you happy?" he asked as he spun me across the brick patio.

"Ecstatically. You?"

"Oh yeah. Especially since I got some news from my doctor today."

"Seriously?"

"Seriously, babe. I'm good to go," he whispered, pulling me tighter into his body. Oh boy. He wasn't lying.

"Well lookie here," I murmured, sneaking a hand down to cop a feel around what was pressing into my thigh. "Um. Wow. You're, like, really, really hard, Simon."

"Hmm? Oh jeez, that's a bottle in my pocket. Literally." He laughed, pulling out a glass bottle from his front pocket and showing it to me. Thank goodness. Not only was he frighteningly hard, the bottle was also . . . hmm . . . how do I say . . . considerably thinner than Simon was.

"Why are you carrying around a bottle?" I asked.

"I thought I'd grab some dirt, maybe from the edge of the dance floor over there, put it with our other bottles. I know it's technically not sand, but there should be something there for tonight."

I grinned and told him it was a very sweet idea. Years ago, Simon had started collecting sand from the beaches he'd visited all over the world, storing them in little labeled bottles and displaying them on a narrow shelf. We'd started a second shelf for beaches we'd visited together. I'd brought some home from the beach where we were married in Vietnam, and I was touched that he'd thought to commemorate tonight as well. But back to his pocket. . . .

"I'm liking where this night is going," I said, deliberately bumping my hips into his, where there was something else taking shape. Definitely bigger than a bottle. "How fast do you think we can get everybody out of here?" I asked, only half joking.

"As soon as the ribs run out they'll leave, right?"

"We are so classy. Serving ribs at our wedding."

"And potato salad. Don't forget the potato salad."

"And pie."

"That pie was great. Never stop making that pie. Dammit, I should have written that into the vows," he said, dipping me low and making me giggle upside down. And there, in our own backyard surrounded by everyone we loved, he kissed me. My husband."

"What a mess."

"I think one of the wedding presents should be cleaning up after," Simon groaned, surveying the damage in the kitchen.

"I don't think that was on our registry, babe," I said sadly, patting him on the shoulder as I walked by to the dining room. Which was still wedding gift central.

"We do, however, have the latest in immersion blenders, electric carving knives, and . . . what the hell is this?" I asked, holding up a white box.

"That's the Mr. Bacon." Simon said proudly.

"Who is mister bacon?"

"No no, Mr. Bacon. You cook bacon in it."

"I gathered that. Why is this necessary?" Every cat in the house had gathered either on the dining room table or underneath. They knew the word *bacon*. They understood the word *bacon*. They loved the bacon.

"You use it to cook bacon in the microwave, easy as pie. Which is appropriate, because if you drape the bacon over this little cup here, you can microwave it into the shape of a little pie. Now you've got a bacon pie thingie that you can fill with other stuff!"

"Who the hell bought us this?"

"Trevor and Megan."

"No way. No way that Megan, a former Food Network gal, gave us this for our wedding."

"Actually, they gave us two presents. They also got us the new white serving dishes you had to have from Williams-Sonoma."

"Atta girl," I praised, and looked once more at the box Simon was now cradling. "Trevor must have gone rogue with that one."

"Keep making fun of my Mr. Bacon. It still doesn't solve the problem of this mess."

"How about a post-wedding-party party? Where we invite many of the same people and put them to work cleaning up? That way we don't have to spend our honeymoon working," I suggested, and Simon's eyes lit up.

"Yeah, why are we spending our wedding night talking about bacon?"

"Well, you were the one that—"

I was silenced by a kiss as Simon crossed the kitchen in two strides, gathered me against him, and pressed his mouth to mine. I ignited instantly.

"You sure about this?" I asked, breathless as he kissed the stuffing out of me.

"You're kidding, right?" he asked, his voice thick and impossibly sexy as he trailed kissed down along my jawline, headed for my neck. Once those lips hit below the chin, I was pretty much done for. "I missed our first wedding night, I'm not missing the second."

"Let's go slow though, okay?" I insisted as he backed me toward the stairs. His doctor had cleared him, sure, but that didn't mean we needed to swing from the chandeliers.

"I like slow," he murmured, gathering a handful of backside.

"We started out slow, you know . . ." I sighed as his lips found my sweet spot just below my ear. We were walking up the stairs now, shutting off lights as we went and kissing like teenagers.

"That's not how I recall it," he said, turning me at the top of the stairs, positioning me in front of him as he walked me down the hallway. His arms were wrapped around my waist and his lips tickled at my ear, making me giggle a bit. I was a little tipsy from beer, but not so tipsy that I was going to be railroaded.

"We did *so* start out slow—we were friends first. Friends for a while, actually," I reminded him, stopping just outside our bedroom door. I leaned in the doorway, keeping him from going inside.

"I don't recall us being friends first. I recall us being something else entirely at first." He nipped at my earlobe. More specifically, at what was hanging from my earlobe. His wedding present to me.

That morning when I woke up, there was a jewelry box sitting on top of the pillow where Simon's head usually was. I could hear him brushing his teeth in the bathroom as I looked around, wondering what he was up to. Since we already felt we'd been married on that beach, there was no "can't see the bride before the wedding," today and I wanted him next to me in our bed.

"What's this?" I asked, scrunching back down into the pillows, tugging the comforter up around me.

"Sahfing for mah brud," was the answer I got.

"I'll wait until you spit, babe," was the answer I gave.

He spit.

He joined me on the bed.

"Just a little something for my bride," he repeated.

"But I thought we weren't doing presents," I protested. We'd discussed it before and agreed that we weren't doing anything special.

"Oh hush up, will you, and open it," he instructed, and I did as I was told.

Blue.

Flashing.

Fire.

Earrings. Drop earrings filled with diamonds and sapphires, exactly the color of his eyes. Teardrop sapphires hung from a delicate diamond-encrusted base.

"Simon, what did you do?" I breathed, my hand shaking.

"I figured this could be the something old, since they're old; the something new, since they're new to you; something blue, obviously; but technically not borrowed, since they're now yours. You're borrowing them permanently."

"From who?" I whispered, already knowing the answer.

"My mom," he replied, and my eyes filled with tears.

"I could not possibly love you more," I told him, bringing him down to me for a sweet kiss.

"You like?"

"I love them."

I promptly put them on, and wore them all day. Which brings me to now, where I had a Wallbanger nibbling on my ear as I stood in a doorway.

"The way I recall it, you hated me on sight that first time we met," he said, switching from my ear to the back of my neck as he held my hair up high.

"I didn't hate you, but I sure wasn't your biggest fan," I admitted, thinking back to him opening his door after I'd been banging at it relentlessly. "I was missing sleep."

"You were missing more than sleep, babe," he said,

nuzzling my shoulder. His hands pulled at my dress, gathering the fabric and bunching it high around my hips. "Pretty sure you were missing this too." And he placed one hand over my sex. Entirely. My body responded as it always did, with full abandon.

"I really *was* missing this," I replied, sinking my hands into his thick, dark hair and twirling it under my fingertips. "But you brought it all back."

"*We* brought it all back," he reminded me, and pushed me into the bedroom.

"We. I like we," I moaned, feeling the bed hit the back of my knees.

Simon and I had never gone this long without sex since we'd been together. And under his hands once more, my body came alive for him. I yanked at his pants as he tugged at my dress. I worried off his shoes as he wriggled me out of my bra. My breasts were full in his hands, heavy, and sensitive. And he took my garter down with his teeth, leaving a trail of openmouthed kisses in his wake.

When we were finally naked, tangled, and panting, I scrambled backward on the bed, moving toward the headboard.

"Where you going, sweet Caroline?" he asked, crawling across the bed to get to me.

"I wanted to hold on for this," I quipped, arching an eyebrow and my back as I grabbed on to the iron headboard.

"That's my girl."

He covered me with his body, all long limbs and strong muscles, as I wrapped my legs around his waist.

"I love you, Simon. I love you so fucking much," I said, sweeping back his hair and holding his face in my hands, his eyes staring down at me.

"I love you too, Mrs. Parker." And then he pressed into me. Our bodies adjusted to each other, remembered each other, uniquely designed to fit perfectly, sinking in and synching up. He held perfectly still for a moment, feeling me wrapped around him in every way.

"Christ, I've missed you," he groaned, his voice strained with the sweet tension of holding back, taking things slow, making sure he was okay.

But that night, our wedding night, we learned the loveliness of taking things exceedingly slow, with precision and quiet effort. Bodies barely moving, sweet sweat collecting between us, adjusting and readjusting, and then coming together quietly in the night.

Quiet.

Slow.

Sweet.

Perfect.

It was romantic and wonderful, our first time as an official married couple.

The second time, however?

Simon couldn't help himself. He brought it on home. Hips thrusting, arms flailing, biting, licking, sucking, fucking. Hands intertwined, then holding fast to the headboard once more.

"You're really going to want to hold on for this one, Nightie Girl."

And he was so very right.

Thump.

"Oh, God."

Thump thump.

"Oh, God."

Good god damn, I loved this man.

And I would continue to for the rest of my life. For *our* lives. Because Wallbanger was the only one who could give me my happy ending.

. . .

. . .

. . .

Ahem.

epilogue

I had heard the Feeder and the Tall One complaining about cleaning up. I did not see the need. After saying the word *bacon* again and again, teasing without any relief, the very least they could do was leave out the remaining rib tips and nibbles from their celebration.

I found a platter that held more than enough tasty treats, and signaled to the girls that I'd hunted up a feast for them. It was my nature to care for those around me, especially my ladies. In return for granting them accommodation in my home, and general protection from repeat offenders like *Hoover* and *disposal* and *garbage truck,* my trio kept me well groomed and well satisfied. If you know what I mean. And I think that you do.

While the ladies were occupied with a particularly tasty hamburger patty, I went back to my earlier search-and-destroy mission. Normally I avoided trash bins, after a misspent youth chasing Q-tips and cotton balls.

Nothing good ever came of those fruitless, albeit fun, pursuits. But something had piqued my interest in one of the upstairs rooms, the one the Feeder and the Tall One used as their litter box.

I walked silently through their sleeping quarters, sensing that they were only lightly dozing. The Tall One had that look about him today, a look I had come to recognize meant the Feeder would be caterwauling throughout the evening. No matter, I had bigger fish to fry. Mmm, fish.

Slipping into their litter box room unnoticed, I went immediately to the trash can. Pawing with delicate grace, I upended the container, spilling the contents onto the floor. Digging through Kleenex, an empty pill bottle, one damnable cotton ball (which I lost at least twenty minutes to, when it decided to run from me), I came upon the curious item.

Wrapped entirely in toilet paper, as if to dissuade me, was an empty box with a long stick inside. The stick was a good weight, balancing nicely in the mouth. It would be good for a game of pounce hockey keep away. Grasping the flat end in my mouth, I padded into the other room and leapt quietly onto the bed. Climbing over legs and knees, elbows and arms, I nestled in between the Tall One and the Feeder, bringing my hockey stick with me for later.

It had been a long day. I'd been up for at least an hour, and sleep was calling. I examined the stick once more, noticing that on one side there was an interesting symbol on one end. Two lines, crossed in the middle. Hmm. Putting the mystery aside for now, I stretched out my legs, making sure I was touching both of my people. It seemed to comfort them. And that was my other job, making sure these two were always comfortable.

I could feel the Tall One beginning to stir; I'd better catch a nap before he was fully awake and bothering the Feeder.

I closed my eyes and slept instantly. Blissful. Happy. Content. For in my dreams, there were rib tips for days . . .

"What the hell is this in the bed? Clive? What did you bring . . . huh."

"What is it?" The Feeder yawned.

A long pause . . .

"Caroline? You want to tell me something?"

A longer pause . . .

"So, Simon. Funny story . . ."

Turn all of your evenings into cocktail hours!

Missed any of the first four intoxicating books
in the Cocktail Series?

Keep reading for sneak peeks!

They're saucy. They're sexy.
They're laugh-out-loud funny.

I'll drink to that!

Caroline doesn't hear things "go bump in the night"—
she hears them go *thump* in the night. And it's always
her new neighbor Simon's headboard . . .

wallbanger

"Caroline, I didn't realize you knew Simon. What a
small world!" Jillian exclaimed, clasping her hands
together.

"I wouldn't say I *know* him, but I'm familiar with his
work," I replied through clenched teeth. Mimi danced
in a circle around us like a little kid with a secret.

"Jillian, you won't believe this but—" she started,
her voice bubbling over with barely concealed mirth.

"Mimi. . . ." I warned.

"Simon is Simon from next door! Simon Wallbanger!" Sophia cried, grasping Benjamin's arm. I'm
sure she only did it so she could touch Benjamin.

"Dammit," I breathed as Jillian took in this
information.

"No fucking way," she breathed, hand clapping over
her mouth after she dropped the f-bomb. Jillian always
tried to be such a lady.

Benjamin looked confused, and Simon had the decency to blush a little.

"Asshole," I mouthed to him.

"Cockblocker," he mouthed back, the smirk returning in full force.

I gasped and clenched my fists, prepared to tell him exactly what he could do with his cockblocker, when Neil burst in.

"Benjamin, check this out—this little hottie here is the Pink Nightie Girl! Can you stand it?" He laughed as Ryan struggled to keep a straight face. Benjamin's eyes widened, and he raised an eyebrow at me. Simon swallowed a laugh.

"Pink Nightie Girl?" Jillian asked, and I heard Benjamin lean in and tell her he'd explain later.

"Okay, that's it!" I shouted, and I pointed at Simon. "You. A word, please?" I barked and grabbed him by the arm. I yanked him outside and pulled him down one of the paths that led away from the house. He scrambled along after me, my heels ringing out angrily on the flagstone.

"Jesus, slow down, will you?"

My response was to dig my nails into his arm, which made him yelp. Good.

We reached a little enclave set away from the house and the party—far enough away that no one would hear him scream when I removed his balls from his body. I released his arm and rounded on him, pointing a finger in his surprised face.

"You've got some nerve telling everyone about me, asshole! What the hell? *Pink Nightie Girl?* Are you kidding me?" I whisper-yelled.

"Hey, I could ask you the same question! Why do all those girls in there call me Wallbanger, huh? Who's telling tales now?" he whisper-yelled right back.

"Are you kidding me? Cockblocker? Just because I refused to spend another night listening to you and your harem does not make me a cockblocker!" I hissed.

"Well, due to the fact that your door banging blocked my cock, it actually *does* make you a cockblocker. Cockblocker!" he hissed back. This entire conversation was beginning to sound like something that might have happened in fourth grade—except for all the nightie and cock talk.

"Now, you listen here, mister," I said, trying for a more adult tone. "I'm not going to spend every night listening to you try to crash your girl's head through my wall with the force of your dick alone! No way, buddy." I pointed a finger at him. He grabbed it.

"What I do on my side of that wall is my business. Let's get that straight right now. And why are you so concerned about me and my dick anyway?" he asked, smirking at me again.

It was the smirk, that damn smirk, that made me go ballistic. That and the fact that he was still holding my finger.

"It *is* my business when you and your sex train come knocking on *my* wall every night!"

"You're really fixated on this, aren't you? Wish you were on the other side of that wall? Are you lookin' to ride that sex train, Nightie Girl?" He chuckled as he wagged his finger in my face.

"Okay, that's it," I growled. I grabbed his finger in defense, which instantly locked us together. We must have looked like two loggers trying to cut down a tree. We struggled back and forth—beyond ridiculous. We both huffed and puffed, each trying to get the upper hand, each refusing to relent.

"Why are you such a manwhoring asshole?" I asked, my face inches from his.

"Why are you such a cockblocking priss?" he asked.

And when I opened my mouth to tell him exactly what I thought, the fucker kissed me.

Caroline and Simon are all set to play house,
but her crazy work schedule and his world travels
keep coming between them and the sheets.
Sure, the reunion sex is hot hot hot—but is
that really enough? Alice Clayton serves
sexy straight up—with a twist.

rusty nailed

As I turned my key in my apartment door I heard a distinct thump, followed by a *click click click* padding toward me.

Clive.

Pushing through the door, I was greeted by my wonder cat, my own little piece of feline heaven. In a burst of gray fur, my ankles were surrounded by purrs and insistent nudges.

"Hi there, sweet boy, were you a good boy today?" I asked, leaning down to scratch his silky fur.

Arching up into my hand, he assured me that yes, he was in fact a sweet boy, and also a good boy. Berating me for leaving him alone for a thousand years, he cooed and chirped, herding me toward the kitchen.

We talked as I readied his dinner for him, which of course I'd been put on earth expressly to do, and our conversation covered the normal subjects. What birds he'd seen from the window today, whether any dust bunnies had emerged from under the bed, and whether I'd find any toys buried in the toe of my slippers. He was noncommittal on this last question.

Once his kibble was in his bowl he ignored me completely, and I headed back to the bedroom to put on some comfy clothes. Untucking my turtleneck, I went to the mirrored dresser to grab some yoga pants. While pulling my arms out of my shirt, my heart leapt into my throat when I saw the reflection of someone sitting on my bed. Instinct kicked in and I whirled, fists clenched, a scream ready to let loose.

My brain only processed that it was Simon after my fist was flung.

"Whoa, whoa, whoa! What the *hell*, Caroline!" he yelled as he grabbed his jaw.

"What the hell Caroline? What the hell *Simon*! What the hell are you doing here?" I yelled back. Good to know if I was ever actually attacked, I wouldn't freeze.

"I came home early to surprise you," he managed, rubbing his jaw and grimacing.

My heart was still racing in my chest, and as I tried to calm down, I noticed the suitcase in the corner. The one I'd missed when I'd come into the room. I looked down and saw the turtleneck still hanging around my neck like a scarf.

"I could just kill you!" I yelled again, charging him and pushing him back onto the bed. "You scared me to death, you idiot!"

"I was planning on calling out to let you know I was here, but then I would've missed that entire conversation with Clive. I didn't want to interrupt." He grinned underneath me, threading his hands around my waist.

I blushed. "Traitor!" I yelled down the hallway. "You could have let me know someone was here—you're a terrible watch-cat!"

A disinterested meow floated back.

"I'm hardly just *someone*. I think I rate a little higher than that," he told the side of my neck, which he was now feathering with the tiniest of kisses. "So, are you going to say hi to your boyfriend who flew all the way across the globe just to show you his hammer, or are you going to punch me again?"

"Not sure yet; I'm still a little freaked out. My heart is literally racing, can you feel that?" I asked, pressing his hand over the left side of my chest.

Only so he could feel my heart. Yep. That's the only reason. Heart was in fact delighted to have Simon home early; she loved a good romantic reunion. Other areas were delighted, as well.

"See now, I thought it was racing because of *me*," he said with a low chuckle, dipping his nose along my collarbone as he "felt my heart."

"Dream on, Wallbanger," I said, feigning indifference. The truth? My heart was now in Simon mode, and it *was* pounding for him. And speaking of pounding.

"So you came home early just to see little ol' me?" I breathed into his ear, sneaking a wet kiss just underneath it. His hands dug a little deeper into my hips as he shifted on the bed.

"I did."

"Think you can help me with this turtleneck?"

"I do."

"And then after that, you wanna show me your hammer?" I asked the front of his T-shirt, nuzzling at him, positioning my legs on either side of him. In answer, he thrust up and let me feel that very hammer. I chuckled. "Mmm, am I gonna get nailed?"

He lifted my turtleneck off, then unsnapped my bra and my breasts tumbled out, causing his eyes to flare, then focus with precision. "No more questions," he directed, sitting up underneath me as he pulled me closer.

I mimed zipping my lips just before he flipped me over onto my back. God, I loved this man.

His lips danced along my collarbone, nipping occasionally with his teeth in a way he always knew got me warm, *fast*. I got it; I'd missed him too. Arching my back, I pressed my breasts against him, twisting and turning to bring me into contact with him as much as I could be, my skin needing to feel his. After a year, he could still bring me to my knees in seconds with one touch, one kiss, one look.

I pushed back against him, flipping us once more and pulling at his jeans. "Off, now," I instructed.

When his belt was gone, his buttons unbuttoned, I pulled apart his jeans to find that once more my man had gone commando.

It's like he was put on earth just to make me come out of my skin.

I snuck one hand inside, grasping him firmly, feeling how warm he was; ready to take me on my own trip around the world.

"Fuck, I missed you," he breathed, his body lean and taut. I slid down the bed, kissing and licking at his skin hungrily. His hands came up to my face, fingers fluttering along my cheekbones, sweeping my hair back. So he could watch.

I took him into my mouth, entirely. His hands clutched at my hair, freezing me in place, holding me exactly how he wanted me. "Mmm, Caroline," he moaned, thrusting ever so slightly. Slightly, my ass—that wasn't how this show was going down.

I pulled back, then took him in again, hard. Using my hands I caressed him, alternating my touch so he never knew quite where I was coming from, using my tongue and mouth to tease and tempt him, coaxing the sweetest dirty words out of that sent-from-heaven mouth of his. That mouth that I knew would exact the sweetest dirty revenge all over my body.

I loved him this way, loved that I could make him this insane. But just before he got too far gone, he pulled me up his body and took my panties off before I could say, hey, those are my panties.

Then he pushed up my skirt, nudging my knees apart with his own. Gazing down at me with those piercing sapphire eyes, he ran his fingers over me, through me, making me groan and moan and shake and shimmy. "So gorgeous like this," he breathed as I cried out.

"Need you, Simon—need you, please!" I was ready to tear my hair off my head and throw it at him, if I thought that would get him inside any faster.

Any further thoughts vanished as he slid home. Thick, hard, and ten kinds of fantastic were all I knew the second Simon pressed inside me. "God, that's amazing," I moaned, the feeling of him filling me over-whelming me.

And when he rolled us so I was on top, and he thrust up hard inside me, it was perfection.

Until afterward, when we lay in a heap of sweaty limbs, and he asked me how I liked his hammer.

Then it was beyond perfection.

Viv Franklin wants to be swept off her feet
by her dream guy, but should she pick the hot cowboy
or the smoldering librarian? This romantic comedy
pits Superman against Clark Kent in a hot and
hilarious battle that promises to rip a bodice or two.

screwdrivered

"Well, well, well."

"Lookee what we have here," I finished, peering up
at Clark from where I sat, stuck.

"I couldn't have said it better myself," he answered,
walking slowly up the porch steps.

When I'd called him, he said he'd be right over. And
he hadn't laughed, just asked if I was all right and did
I need anything. I told him a margarita would be nice.
He'd ignored that request, but he had brought his toolbox. Rubbermaid. Red. Stamped with Clark Barrow on
the side—in case someone tried to take it?

Sunday Evening Clark was much more dressed
down: faded jeans, running shoes, untucked plaid shirt
over a white undershirt. I suddenly said a prayer that it
wasn't a tank-top undershirt, that he was the kind of guy

who wore T-shirts, and then mentally slapped myself for giving a shit what he wore under his faded plaid shirt. That looked soft and comfortable and warm. I shivered. It was getting cold out here, playing buoy on the sea of porch.

He knelt down in front of me and assessed the situation.

"One would think it unwise, Vivian, knowing the condition of this rotten wood, to traipse about so carelessly," he said as he poked at the wood around my left leg, which was buried to midthigh. I'd been sitting half on and half off the broken floorboard for the better part of twenty minutes, and was starting to get more than a little agitated.

"One would think that after getting punched in the nose one would be unwise to provoke me," I said sweetly.

He turned his gaze from my leg to my face, his eyes calculating. "You're the one stuck in the porch. You sure you want to pick a fight with me right now?"

He had me there, dammit. "Okay, fine. No fight picking. But do *something,* Clark."

"I'm waiting for the magic word."

"Um, now?"

"Really?"

"Asshole?"

"Come on."

"Clark!"

"Vivian."

"Oh, fine. *Please* help me, Clark. Please, please, please?" I managed, gritting my teeth.

"That wasn't so bad, was it?" he smiled, his face lighting up.

"Still not out of this porch here," I said.

He nodded. "As personally gratifying as it is to see you like this, there is a bit of storm coming and I'd rather not be out here when it hits. So let's see what we can do here, shall we?"

"Yes, shall we?" I repeated, leaning back so he could get a better look at how I was wedged.

"Pardon me, I need to get a little closer here. I just— Ah, yes, I can see it there." Clark had leaned across me, one arm on either side of me as he peered through the broken board to the ground below. His head was almost flush with the floor. And flush with what else was on the floor. Flush with my— Oh my. I unexpectedly felt his breath on my bare thighs. I was dressed in running shorts that left little to the imagination, and *my* imagination was bombarding my senses with the most inappropriate images.

All I could think about was if he just moved about three inches to the left, he could probably get me off with his jaw alone. And how in world had I never noticed that it was so very strong, so very chiseled, so very lightly covered with Sunday-evening stubble? Stubble that could so very easily drag back and forth across the inside of my legs, up and down, and right and left, and then up, up, and away toward my—

"I'm going to have to go down," he said, and it took all the strength I had not to bury my hand in that flippy soft brown hair and take him at his word.

"Sorry?" I asked, panting. I was panting, for Christ's sake! Over a librarian?

Mmmm, over *a librarian* . . .

"I have to go down beneath the porch. Believe me, I'm not looking forward to it. Who knows what's under there?" he said, turning toward me. All I could see was bandage, and the bruises that were fading from purple to yellow around the edges, and the spell was broken.

Still breathing a little heavy, I warned him to watch out for dolls. And watched as he hurried down the steps, around the side of the house, and began removing the latticework cover on the side of the porch with the utmost care.

What the hell! Lusting after a librarian, when there was a cowboy on the loose? It was clear that lusting after Hank had addled my brains. I was seeing things, imagining things, getting hot over the slightest touch, even from a guy like Clark.

The wind blew more forcefully across the porch, and I shivered. What the hell was taking so long?

"Hey! You want to put a little hustle on over there?" I finally called out, when the third piece of lattice was placed carefully onto the porch.

His head popped up over the edge. "Do you have any idea how old this is?"

"Do you have any idea how much it's going to suck if you're caught underneath there in the rain?"

He looked at the sky, getting darker by the minute. "Point taken." He pried off the last of the lattice, then disappeared.

I could hear scrambling coming from beneath me, and then I could feel the ground shifting a little under my stuck foot.

"Vivian? It's just me. Don't be alarmed."

"No kidding, Clark. Who else would it be?"

"Well, pardon me all over the place. I was just concerned that if you were surprised, your first instinct would be to kick. So let's see what we can do about getting this free."

Then he put his hands on my leg. Wrapped his hands around my ankle, turning it slightly. "Okay, it's wedged into a cement block, but I think I can get it loose. Bear with me a moment, Vivian."

"It's Viv. And be careful, huh?" I called down.

"Impossible woman," he muttered. His hands traveled a little farther up my leg, inside, and then around the back of my knee. And then I felt . . . well, it felt like . . .

"Clark! Did you just lick—"

"*No!*" he yelled, wrenching my foot free at that exact moment and pushing it up through the porch. I fell backward, my leg pulling clear of the wood and my heart pounding. I saw him crawl out from beneath the porch, dust himself off, and then walk toward me.

I pointed at him. "You licked my leg."

"I did nothing of the kind," he said. But the tips of his ears were red.

Flap-flap-flap-flap.

"Ah crap, I forgot about that."

"You're kind of a two-crisis girl, aren't you?" He laughed, reaching behind his toolbox and picking up a lacrosse stick.

"*That's* what you brought to kill a bat?"

"It was either this or my squash racket." He took a few practice swipes at the air. "Besides, we're not going to kill it. We're going to catch it, then let it go."

"There is no *we*. There's a *you,* as in *you* are going to get the bat!"

"It's your house, you should be helping me," he said. "And for someone who acts so tough, you sure are scared of a little thing like a bat."

"I'm not scared!"

When he had the nerve to make a bowing gesture, as if to say *well then, go ahead on in without me,* I grumbled, "Okay fine—I'm a little scared. I'll help you, but you're going in first." I stood up and brushed off my shorts. I now had another scrape to match the one on the other leg. *Honestly.*

I rummaged in the garage until I found a rake and a bucket, then rejoined Clark on the porch. Stepping over the hole, I huddled behind him as he opened the front door. We went inside, alert and listening.

"Is something burning?" he asked, sniffing the air.

"Dammit, my dinner!" I wailed, rushing past him and into the kitchen. "Motherfucker!"

"Vivian!" Clark exclaimed, hurrying past me to turn off the burners.

Smoke billowed from the oven, my chicken breasts now charred beyond recognition. Rice? Now a cake in the bottom of the pan. And the vegetables? Crust. I started throwing the pots into the sink, probably slamming them a little harder than necessary. I was pissed at the porch, pissed at the house, pissed that my leg hurt, and pissed off that I still had a bat in the house. *A bat in the house!*

"Were you expecting someone for dinner?" Clark asked from the doorway to the dining room. His face looked tight—hurt?

I glanced past him and saw the candles burning on the table. "No, that was just for me," I replied, pushing past him and blowing out the candle.

"You lit candles just to eat alone?"

"Yeah. So?" I asked, turning back to him. I saw the bat. It was perched on the lacrosse stick, just behind his head.

"Oh. Boy. Um, Clark?"

"I think if you want to light candles, even if it's just you, that's perfectly okay," Clark said.

"Right. Agreed. But right now? You need to—"

"I mean, after all, if you don't think you're good company, no one else will, right?"

"Totally. Can I just—"

"I eat most of my meals alone too, although I've never thought about lighting candles. Not sure a guy doing it would be seen as being quite as empowering as it is for a girl, rather sad actually. But good for you, Vivian. Light a candle even if it's just chicken or—"

"Duck."

"Yes, even if it's—"

"Fucking *duck*, Clark!" I yelled, lunging in with my rake and swatting at the bat.

Clark hit the deck and I knocked the bat off the back of the lacrosse stick. "Bucket! Bucket!" I yelled, and he slid it across the floor. Slamming it down on the bat, I sat on top of it, giving a war cry. "Wahoooooo!" In victory, I lifted the rake high over my head—where it caught in the chandelier and damn near ripped the entire thing out.

And as it hung from the ceiling, swinging back and forth, I sat on a bucket in the middle of my dining room, with a bat under my butt, and a librarian under the table.

Cue lightning and thunder.

Cue crashing rain.

There was nothing I could do but laugh.

Take one former Miss Golden State, one hot
veterinarian, twenty rescue pit bulls, moonlight,
a stack of old records with Frank Sinatra crooning
about strangers in the night, and shake well!
And did we mention the pit bulls?

mai tai'd up

Lucas came in the front door of the animal hospital
with a bag over his shoulder and a cup of coffee in his
hand. "Hey, Chloe," he said, smiling and stopping just a
few inches from me. "Morning, Marge."

"Hey, Lucas, how's your day going?" I asked, turning
from Marge slightly to look at him, which meant looking up at him. Fudge, this guy was tall; it surprised me
almost every time I was around him. "I see you got your
scrubs washed in time for work today."

"I'm barely here on time; I overslept. You wore me
out yesterday." He groaned, rotating his shoulders a bit.

"Me!" I exclaimed, massaging his left shoulder.
"You're the one that wanted to keep going; I was good
after twenty minutes. Especially once I found that sweet
spot." I smiled.

"Yeah, but admit it. You loved it."

"Oh, yeah. Totally worth the soreness today. But next time we should stretch afterward."

"Agreed. By the way, you left this in the back of my truck yesterday," he said, pulling my bikini top out of the bag on his shoulder.

"Oh, thanks, that was thoughtful. I wondered where that went."

Marge's head exploded in a cloud of Jean Naté confetti. "What the . . . But when did . . . Now wait just a—"

The two of us grinned at each other, perfectly aware of what we'd just said and how it sounded.

"See you tonight?" I asked, and he gave me a slow nod.

"Wouldn't miss it," he murmured, his voice low and full of promise. "You headed home now?"

"Mm-hmm." I nodded also, just as slowly. I pursed my lips. He licked his. Marge sighed dreamily, and I had to cough to cover up a laugh. "Walk me to my car?"

"I thought you'd never ask." Setting his bag and coffee on the front desk, he guided me out the front door with his hand in the small of my back. Not pushing, just the warmth of his skin telling me which way to go.

"See ya, Marge," I called over my shoulder, then rested my head on his bicep for good measure. We could hear her sputtering halfway out into the parking lot. "I think we just made her day," I cackled, collapsing against the side of the clinic.

"I don't know how you kept it together. I thought for sure I was going to lose it when you started in with the sweet spot."

"Well, that's typically when everyone loses it," I quipped, and he groaned. We took a moment to compose ourselves, and then started to walk over to my car.

"So, tonight?"

"What about tonight?" I asked, wiping a tear from my eye, still chuckling a bit.

"Pretty sure you just insinuated back there that we had plans for tonight."

"I did?"

"You said, and I quote, 'see you tonight,' " he said. "In a very Marilyn Monroe voice too, which was a nice touch, by the way," he said.

"Oh, yeah, I guess I did," I mused. "Well, we don't really have to do anything. It was mainly for effect, just to mess with her a bit."

"While I always love an opportunity to mess with Marge, I'd hate to make us liars. What time should I come over?"

"Come over?"

"You said it, sister. Now you plan it," he replied, pointing at me. "It'll be hard to top paddleboarding, but try."

There was that twinkle again. You'd think a guy that twinkles as much as he does wouldn't get to me, but boy . . . this guy's twinkle had some voodoo magic.

"I can't promise anything as elaborate as paddleboarding, but how about dinner? Should be a nice night; we could grill and sit out on the patio?"

"Done. Six thirty?"

"Done."

And with that, a plan was made. And he was keeping his promise: those nights and weekends were getting filled.

Speaking of getting filled . . .

No one was speaking of getting filled!

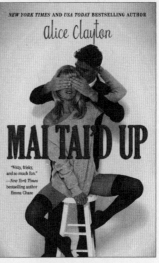